FASTER THAN FAST

Colter stood in front of Yeager and said, "You tried to bushwack me. Maybe you'd like to finish the job."

Yeager was a pro. He lived by his gun. Now he gave Colter a close look and saw that Colter's holster wasn't tied low like a gunslinger's would be. Yeager grinned. Colter was just a thirty-dollar-a-month cowhand looking for trouble, nothing to worry about.

Yeager reached for his gun and felt even more confident as it began to clear leather a fraction of a second before Colter made his move.

He didn't notice that the big Colt .45 had magically appeared in Colter's hand until he heard the explosion of the shot and felt a hammer blow against his chest as a 255 grain soft lead bullet ripped into his heart.

Yeager was the first in town to make a mistake about Colter. He wouldn't be the last. . . .

COLTER

Quint Wade

A SIGNET BOOK

NEW AMERICAN LIBRARY

PUBLISHER'S NOTE

This book is a work of fiction. Names, characters, places, and
incidents are either the product of the author's imagination or are
used fictitiously, and any resemblance to actual persons, living
or dead, events, or locales is entirely coincidental.

SIGNET TRADEMARK REG. U.S. PAT. OFF. AND FOREIGN COUNTRIES
REGISTERED TRADEMARK—MARCA REGISTRADA
HECHO EN CHICAGO, U.S.A.

SIGNET, SIGNET CLASSIC, MENTOR, ONYX, PLUME,
MERIDIAN and NAL BOOKS are published by
NAL PENGUIN INC.,
1633 Broadway, New York, New York 10019

First Printing, May, 1988

1 2 3 4 5 6 7 8 9

PRINTED IN THE UNITED STATES OF AMERICA

1

Colter lay belly down at the foot of a crag that jutted fifty feet into the still Arizona air, waiting. Somewhere below him in the arroyo that cut through the desert's rough surface were two Chiricahua Apaches. He'd caught a quick glimpse of them trailing him earlier and had managed to shake them for a while. But he knew that one doesn't lose Chiricahua trackers for long. He'd have to fight, and being on ground of his own choosing was an advantage.

The sunbaked butte behind him was ideal for back cover. It was broad and tall and had a steep sheer face that bulged out slightly at the bottom before it angled back sharply, making an undercut. The base curved like a bent bow so that both ends were visible with very little twisting of the head.

Colter blew a short upward blast of air across the tip of his nose to rid himself of the drop of perspiration that hung there. It was hot, and though the sun had reached the top of the crag, throwing a shadow over his waist and legs, the sand beneath him was scorching. He smelled the stale sweat of his body mingled with the odor of tobacco, horse, and ironwood smoke that was part of him. Peering through the slender branches of a creosote bush, he blinked to keep the sweat from his eyes. Then, readjusting his shoulders to gain what little protection from the blazing sun the small plant offered, he wiped the palm of his right hand on his shirtfront and thumbed the hammer of his Winchester back to the firing position.

A buzzard wheeled in the brassy sky silhouetted against a distant cirrus cloud. Colter's dark eyes flicked from the bird to the ridge beyond the arroyo where junipers offered small patches of shade. Then they moved quickly down the face of the ridge, among the broken boulders that squatted along its flank, through a stand of agaves with their clusters of yellow tufted blossoms, and passed several lonely saguaros. Continuing, he glanced rapidly in zigzag fashion across a ground cover of snakeweed to the rim of the arroyo. Nothing moved. The Apaches were masters at waiting. The price of survival in the desert was patience. Often the first to move was the first to die.

Colter watched a cactus wren about to land in an arrowweed bush suddenly veer sharply to the right. His eyes narrowed. Digging his elbow deeper into the sand, he cradled the barrel of his Winchester in his left hand and fired two quick rounds at the bush, spacing the shots six inches apart. He heard the thud of bullets hitting flesh followed by a short gasp. The arrowweed moved violently and a brown hand thrust into view, the fingers clawing as they dug spasmodically into the sand. Colter waited. The cactus wren, driven to a new perch by the firing of the Winchester, squawked and fluttered its wings. Colter looked once more at the brown hand. The clawing had stopped.

Again his eyes swiftly covered the area. Every rock, bush, and shadow was read in a moment's glance. He knew he was being watched, but he saw nothing, and to see nothing when danger was there bothered him.

His horse whinnied and stamped nervously. Something was spooking him. Colter wondered if the remaining Chiricahua had somehow managed to get into the arroyo near the horse. He left the cover of the creosote bush and worked his way toward the spot where the roan paced at the end of its tether. As Colter reached the edge of the ravine, the gelding looked up and whinnied again softly, then stopped its pacing. Colter felt uneasy. The unknown position of the second Chiricahua plagued him. Then his stomach began to tighten. It was the same feeling he'd had on several occasions when he'd looked down the open barrel of a gun while the man on the other end thumbed the hammer back.

He leaped into the arroyo an instant before a bullet kicked a handful of sand into the air from the spot where he'd just squatted. He moved quickly down the gully a dozen yards toward the direction from which the shot had come. Using the cover of a smokethorn shrub that grew from the bottom of the wash, he peered through its blue-tipped branches and waited. Then a faint sound drifted his way, the sound of muffled metallic scratching. Quickly he put together the faint clicking and the unmistakable sound of the rifle that had fired at him. They fit into a pattern he'd seen and heard before. The rifle shot had sounded like a Springfield, and if he was right, the scratching sound was made by the Chiricahua trying to dig the expanded cartridge case out of the breach. He'd known men, friends of his, who'd lost their lives when their Springfields had jammed at a crucial time. Some of Custer's troops had suffered the same fate. Without waiting he crawled over the top of the arroyo and stood for an instant. The high vantage point allowed him to spot the Indian at the same time the Chiricahua saw him. As Colter snapped a quick shot from hip high, the startled Apache dropped the rifle and leaped between two boulders, disappearing in an instant.

Colter levered a new shell into the breech of his Winchester and advanced cautiously. He knew that Chiricahua seldom carried a hand gun and that the Indian would now be armed only with a knife. Upon reaching the spot where the brave had been a moment earlier, he glanced down at the rifle. It was a .45-70 trapdoor Springfield with a brass cartridge case jammed in its breech. He edged around the boulders but saw nothing. Then, keeping a wary eye, he moved back toward the arroyo.

A rattler buzzed somewhere in the brush off to his right. Colter turned toward the sound in time to see the Chiricahua already in the air, knife in hand, completing a leap that would bring the Indian crashing down on top of him in another instant. Colter dropped to his left knee and drove the stock of his Winchester upward in a hard blow. The metal butt plate caught the warrior in the ribs, snapping two of the bones. The power of the thrust, coupled with his own momentum, twisted the Indian's body in midair and sent him crashing head and shoulders onto a small ridge of volcanic rock. He lay stunned for a moment.

Thrown off balance by the leverage he'd applied to the Apache's body, Colter fell back heavily in the sand. The Chiricahua rose to a crouching position first and shook the dizziness from his head. Then, spotting his opponent in the act of getting to his feet, he *leaped* with his knife raised and ready. Unable to swing the Winchester into action, Colter's hand dropped to his holster, and in one blinding move, he palmed his Colt, fired, and rolled to a new position. A round bluish hole appeared in the Chiricahua's forehead a fraction of a second before he hit the sand where Colter had lain.

Colter rose to his feet. There was no need to roll the Indian over and check for signs of life. The back of his skull had been blown away and dark-red blood oozed through the thick hair to be soaked up eagerly by the parched earth that was to be his hunting ground no longer. Colter knew that there would be no fires in the slain Chiricahua's wickiups that evening and he felt a sadness. Many of their ways made more sense to him than those of the culture he called his own. Things were happening that bothered him. Some of the Apaches had left the reservation choosing to follow their brilliant leader, Vittorio. Fires burned in the council lodges and there was much unrest. The whole border area was beginning to stir uneasily. Colter didn't like it, but then no one had asked his opinion. But right now his first concern was to stay alive and get to Charleston and find out how his brother Jack had been killed; also Jack's ranch would need tending to. One hundred and sixty acres wasn't much as cattle ranches went in the West, where some totaled more than a million acres, but it needed looking after.

He walked to where his gelding stood watching him intently. "Let's go, boy. We've had enough trouble for the day."

A thin layer of sky separated the sun from the peaks of the Pinal Mountains when Colter finally reined to a halt. He had just enough time to find a flat place to sleep before the sun settled beyond the mountain's rim, taking its warmth with it. He unsaddled the roan and tethered it in a patch of mesquite grass. Then, after he'd spread out his bedroll, he had a cold supper of hardtack and jerky. It was the same unappetizing meal he'd eaten for the last week. The cans of tomatoes he'd brought helped out the first couple of days, but they hadn't lasted long. He wanted some coffee badly but dismissed the thought of building an evening fire with so many Apaches roving around. Days had passed since he'd eaten a real sit-down supper, and that pleasure was still a good two days away.

He propped his head against his saddle and rolled a cigarette, spilling a few strands of Bull Durham on his shirt. Taking a deep puff, he let the tension ease from his long frame without losing the vigilance so needed to survive on the desert. His thoughts drifted ahead to Charleston as they had each evening since he'd received a telegram saying his brother Jack was dead. It had been signed by a Miss Cynthia Dobbs, which had surprised him. He sure didn't know anyone by that name, and he expected a telegram like that to have been signed by the sheriff or the town marshal. Neither he nor Jack was much of a hand at writing and they hadn't kept up. He wondered what kind of a woman Cynthia Dobbs was. It was hard to picture her, with nothing more than a name to go by. He also wondered if she'd been the cause of Jack's death. Jack had been forced to leave Texas three years earlier for shooting a man because of a woman. It was a fair fight, but the man was well-liked and Jack wasn't, so he'd been told to leave the state and not return again unless he wanted trouble. Colter ran his fingers along the stubble of his beard. Killing a man in self-defense was something anyone might be forced to do at one time or another. He wondered if Jack had died in a fair fight. He'd find out as soon as he got to Charleston.

He finished his cigarette and stubbed it out on the ground next to his bedroll. A pack of coyote cubs yapped and made feeble attempts at howling somewhere in the darkness behind him. Soon the strong voice of an adult overrode the yipping of the cubs and set off a string of howls that seemed to reach for miles. Colter stretched and yawned. Then, inhaling deeply, he smiled. He liked the night sounds and the pleasant aroma of the arrowweed. The desert got to a man, if he didn't have to fight Apaches or drive cattle across it. He took out his .45 and brought it up under the blankets near his head. Still gripping it, he closed his eyes, and with that special ability that few men have, he went to sleep almost immediately.

The pale light of dawn was just beginning to outline Maple Peak to the east as Colter awoke, not with a start, but instantly alert. He threw the blankets off and slipped his .45 back into its holster. After he'd tied up his bedroll, he took his tooled California saddle and swung it up on the roan's back and tightened the cinch. Then he mounted and took one last look at his camp. Satisfied that he'd left no sign, he nudged the roan into an easy gallop. He was headed for Charleston. There were questions that needed answering, questions that Colter had been thinking of for the last week, and when he asked questions, few men or women had the courage to refuse an answer.

Toward midafternoon his roving glance caught the sharp ridge of a sandstone outcropping off to his left and he halted. He knew that water oftentimes collected where clay and sandstone met, forming a pool above the clay and alongside the layer of sandstone. If that layer were broken, there might be a spring there. He needed water badly and so did his horse.

Colter relaxed the reins and the gelding moved forward at a trot, sensing the water ahead. When he reached the spring, he dismounted and tied the roan to a *yerba del pasmo* bush. Then he picked several of the twigs from the broomlike shrub and put them in his shirt pocket. He knew the Apaches chewed them for toothaches. A man could never tell when he'd need medicine like that out in the desert. He bellied down and drank slowly, raising his head now and then to breathe and then immersing his face to drink again. After filling his canteen, he tied it behind the cantle.

The big gelding stamped impatiently as Colter untied the tether and loosened the cinch. Then it moved eagerly to the waterhole, where it drank noisily, clanking its bit with every mouthful of the cool liquid. Colter splashed water on his face and raised big handfuls to the nape of his neck. After beating the dust from his shirt, he brought out his tobacco and rolled a cigarette. He wanted to relax, take off his boots, and soak his feet, but the dust cloud he'd seen earlier needed checking.

A light scratching sound brought him whirling around with his gun drawn. It was a large chuckwalla with a hairy tail scrambling over a rock. Colter watched it stop under the lip of the stone and settle itself into a small crevice where it puffed out its sides with air to wedge in tightly. He grinned and holstered his gun. If it were evening, he'd sharpen a stick and puncture that lizard. They were good eating and he was hungry, but now wasn't the time.

Colter climbed over the lip where the chuckwalla lay bloated and reached the top of the outcropping. He remained there for nearly half an hour but saw nothing. Must have been a dust devil, he decided. He tightened the cinch and swung into the saddle. Then he nudged the gelding gently in the flank. Feeling somewhat better from the cool water and green grass, it broke into an easy lope.

During the rest of the day, Colter saw no sign of Apaches. By early morning the following day, he reached the banks of the San Pedro River. After the gelding had taken him across, he took the saddle off and let the big horse laze around in the water while he rinsed the sweat and the desert from his clothes. After some hardtack and his final piece of jerky, he saddled up for the last twenty-five miles to Charleston.

When he'd ridden for several hours, he stopped on the crest of a rise to let the gelding breathe. In the distance lay Charleston.

"It can't be more than five miles now boy," he said, patting the roan's neck. "I think we made it."

He stood up in the stirrups and stretched, then relaxed and rolled a cigarette. After lighting up, he started down the slope. Just as he reached the bottom, he caught a slight movement of something up ahead. By pure reflex he touched the rein to the gelding's neck and it turned instantly. At that moment Colter felt a stabbing blow in his shoulder that knocked him from the saddle. It was followed immediately by the crack of a rifle shot.

As he hit the dirt, he rolled behind the base of a saguaro for cover and drew his .45. He could see a man wearing a sugarloaf sombrero moving cautiously toward him with his rifle ready.

A barrel cactus prevented Colter from getting a clear shot at the stranger. He pressed his hand against the wound in his shoulder and felt the hole the slug had torn. The big gelding edged over toward its master and whinnied. It stopped between him and the bush-whacker, further blocking Colter's vision. Just before the man reached the gelding, Colter fired beneath the horse's belly. The slug tore upward into the stranger's thigh. He dropped his rifle and grabbed the horn of Colter's saddle. The stranger's quick movement coming from the horse's right side spooked him and sent him galloping off with the man hanging on to the saddle horn. He bounced along, legs dragging the brush, for a few yards, then let go and fell heavily to the ground. He staggered to his feet and stumbled into a cluster of rocks.

In a few moments Colter heard a horse take off at a gallop. He got unsteadily to his feet and whistled for the gelding. When it trotted up, he tried to pull himself into the saddle. He could feel his strength slipping and his hand let go. He spun against the horse's flank and crumpled to the ground.

2

Amos Carson lifted the hat from his large shaggy head and pulled his index finger like a blade across the breadth of his forehead, collecting the perspiration and flicking it off in one quick movement. Then, after running his hand through his matted gray hair, he put the hat back on and readjusted the brim against the piercing rays of the noonday sun.

The mule was trying his patience again. It stood sullen and angry, waiting for a chance to kick him. Amos swung his heavy hand like a chunk of oak smacking the mule smartly on the haunch.

"Git over, you splayfooted knothead." Then he glanced over at his golden-haired son. "Johnny, hook up the other end of this whiffletree."

Johnny sat hunched over the edge of the horse trough trying to flip a stinkbug on its back with a long stick.

"Johnny!" Amos bellowed. "You gonna sit there like a big-ass robin or you gonna hook up this whiffletree so we can drive out yonder and git that firewood?"

Johnny leaped in the air like he'd been stung. "I . . . I . . . I was playin', Pa. I'll hook up that firewood."

Amos shook his head and sighed. "You're a good boy, Johnny," he said softly, "but hod damn you're a dumb one."

He lit his pipe again while he watched Johnny take

the traces in his big hands and hook them to the sin-
gletree. Each movement the boy made was painfully
slow and methodical, his face screwed up in concentration. He was a big boy for eighteen and stronger
than most. In many ways Johnny appeared fine. The
accident had left only a thin scar running across the
back of his skull from the bottom of one ear to the top
of the other one. The slack jaw and vacant stare, however, gave his face the unmistakable mark of the men-
tal incompetent. His sloping hunched shoulders and
the way his arms swung with the palms facing the rear
completed the picture. Amos had continued to hope
for a while that Johnny would fully recover from his
injury, but in thirteen years little light had penetrated
the dark regions of the boy's mind, a mind that had
been so alert and eager to learn during those first five
years. Amos tapped the bowl of his pipe against the
steel rim of the wagon wheel as Johnny straightened
up.

"I did it, Pa," the boy said slowly.

"You shore did, son. Did a good job, too," Amos
commented.

Johnny grinned. "We goin' now?"

"Yeah, hop on!"

Johnny let the tailgate down and sat on the back of
the bed so he could drag the toes of his boots along
the center ridge between the wheel ruts and kick at the
little piles of dried sheep dung along the way.

When they'd gone about a mile, Amos pulled up and
cupped his hand behind his ear. "You hear that, Johnny? You hear that rifle shot?"

"Huh?"

"I said you hear a rifle shot?" Amos repeated

"Don't hear nothin'," Johnny said.

"I don't mean now. I meant 'fore I stopped."

A pistol shot echoed across the flats.

"Yeah," Johnny said. "Yeah . . . It's a rifle. It's a-shootin'."

"That ain't no rifle. It's a pistol," Amos corrected. "First one I heered was a buffalo gun."

"They a-shootin' buffalo?" Johnny got off the tailgate.

"Ain't no buffalo in these parts, but somebody's sure as hell shootin' at somethin' on the other side of that ridge. Git on."

Johnny jumped back on the wagon and moved up next to Amos on the driver's seat. Just as they reached the head of the ridge, a rider wearing a sugarloaf sombrero streaked by.

"Looks like he's got the devil on his tail, don't it?" Amos said. "A man ridin' like that's gittin' away from somethin'. Let's take a look."

Colter's big roan took several steps toward the two of them as the wagon pulled up. Amos got down and took the gelding's reins.

"Here, tie him to the tailgate, Johnny, while I take a look at this feller."

He opened Colter's shirt and checked the wound in his shoulder. Then he rolled him on his side and ripped the shirt away. Red pieces of raw meat flapped loosely round the jagged hole the slug had torn in Colter's back. "Good Lord almighty! Look at the size of that hole. You could stuff a prairie chicken in that thing."

"Is he dead, Pa?" Johnny asked, coming up.

"He ain't more than a lick away," Amos answered. "Good thing he's a big 'un. A shot like that would kill most men. We'd best git him back to the cabin."

"Found a gun," Johnny said, holding the rifle up.

Amos took the Sharps from Johnny and turned it over slowly to inspect it. He shook his head knowingly. "Yeah, that's what done it. Where'd you find this?"

"Over yonder. The horse . . . he was a-standin' on it."

"Well, put it in the wagon and then give me a hand. If this feller makes it, he'll be wantin' to know who that gun belongs to, and maybe we can help him catch the bastard."

When they reached the cabin, Colter was carried inside and put on Amos' bed.

"You go into town and fetch the doctor and mind you don't say nothin' about this here stranger. Tell him . . . tell him I cut myself with an ax. You hear?"

Johnny looked blank. "Yeah . . . with an ax. Did you hurt yourself, Pa?"

Amos nodded. "Shore did. Now remember what I told you, and if he ain't there, don't wait more than a half an hour. And don't talk to nobody."

Johnny was excited when he rode off toward Charleston. He rarely got to go into town himself.

Amos watched him leave, then turned back to Colter once again. Something had to be done to stop the flow of blood. He took the knife he'd found tucked under Colter's belt and put the blade into the fire to heat. Then he unsaddled the roan, turned it out in the corral, and carried Colter's saddle into the house. After he'd applied the hot knifeblade to cauterize the wound, he bandaged it as best he could.

Then he drew from his pocket the telegram he'd found in Colter's saddlebags.

"So you're Jack Haines' brother, eh?" he said softly. "Well, looks to me like you was expected." He put the telegram back in the saddlebag and then tamped some tobacco into his pipe.

It was a couple of hours before Johnny rode in. He was by himself.

"Doc wasn't there, Pa," he said, dismounting.

"I kinda figured that," Amos replied. "I'll bet you

four bits to a buffalo chip he was out at the Bar K. Did the doc's missus say where he'd gone?''

"Yeah . . . he was gone . . . a-fixin' somebody's leg out at Mr., ah, Mr., ah. . . ''

"Kittleman," Amos said, supplying the name.

"Yeah," Johnny said, glowing as though he'd thought of it.

"I knowed it," Amos thundered. "That backshootin' sidewinder we seen hightailin' it out of the draw was one of Kittleman's hands."

"Yeah," Johnny said, "Kittleman."

"It wasn't Kittleman," Amos corrected. "It was that bean-belly they call Yeager. Ain't nobody else I know of wears one of them Mexican sombreras. This feller here will be mighty pleased to find out who blowed a hole in him."

"Ain't he gonna die, Pa?"

"Ain't dead yet, but I shore don't know why."

"We gonna take him to town, Pa?" Johnny asked.

"No, we're gonna put him in the storeroom. I figure some of Kittleman's boys will be nosin' around purty quick to see if Yeager done his job right. If they don't find this feller out in that draw where we picked him up, they'll be lookin' here first thing. I'll move some of that stuff out of the road in there, and you bring in some hay."

The storeroom was a long low addition built onto the rear of the house. It had a sloping roof whose trailing edge was some four feet off the ground. There were no windows in it, and it had only one opening; a blanket-covered doorway reached from the main room of the cabin.

Amos was breathing hard by the time they'd finished carrying Colter in. "Now," he said, straightening up, "take this feller's horse and tie him the other side of them big rocks back of the sheep pen. Then unhitch the mules and put 'em in the corral. Better put yore horse in there too,'' Amos ordered. ''We want ever'-thing to look settled.''

While Johnny was tending to the team, Amos put the California saddle under the bed and then cleared away the bloody shirt he'd removed while doctoring Colter's wound.

Johnny came running in very excited. ''They's some horses a-comin', Pa.''

Amos went to the door and peered out. ''You'd better stay next to me and don't say nothin'. You understand. Nary a word. I'll do whatever talkin' is necessary.'' He picked up a double-barrel shotgun and stepped outside as the four riders reined to a halt in the yard before the cabin. The leader was Duke, burly foreman of the Bar K. Amos checked the others; Curly Bill, Joe, and one man he'd never seen before.

Duke spoke. ''Ain't seen no stranger ridin' through, have you, sheepherder?'' The last word was said with obvious contempt.

''I ain't seen nothin' stranger than you four dudes in a month of Sundays,'' Amos replied. Duke leaned forward as though about to dismount. Amos cocked both barrels of his shotgun and grinned. Duke sat back in the saddle again. ''And if I did,'' Amos continued, ''I shore as hell wouldn't come a-runnin' to you about it.''

''Feisty old goat, ain't he?'' Curly Bill said.

Johnny chuckled.

''How about you, Junior,'' Duke said to Johnny. ''You seen a stranger around lately?''

Johnny just grinned.

''I said we ain't seen nobody,'' Amos answered.

''I'm talkin' to the dummy, old man. He can understand, can't he?'' Duke mocked.

Amos raised the shotgun so the barrels pointed directly at the layer of fat that hung over Duke's belt. ''He does a hell of a lot better than you do, fat gut,'' he snapped. ''Now, 'less you want me to blow about forty pounds of lard offen that ass of yourn, you'd best turn tail and git the hell off my land.''

"That thing's only got two shots, and there's four of us, sheepherder." Duke sneered.

"You want to be the first?" Amos asked. "How about you, Curly? Joe?" No one moved. Curly swallowed dryly.

Duke had been called and he knew it. "You're gettin' a little too big for your britches, old man," he said. "We don't like sheepherders around here, you know."

"You ain't got brains enough to like nothin' Kittleman don't tell you to like," Amos growled. "Now git goin' 'fore I lose my temper."

Johnny laughed and slapped his thigh.

As the others headed out of the yard, Duke made one last comment, "Mr. Kittleman ain't gonna like your attitude, sheepherder. He ain't gonna like it one bit. And I'll tell you somethin' else, old man. I don't like it either. You'll go too far one of these days, and that'll be it."

"I've heered geese fart before," Amos growled.

Duke turned his sorrel and spurred it savagely in the flank. When he'd ridden out of range of Amos' shotgun, he yanked on the reins and the sorrel skidded to a halt. Drawing his .45, he shot a gentle old ewe that stood suckling her lamb off the side of the trail, then galloped off to catch up with the others.

The lamb nudged its dead mother and bleated.

Amos repressed the urge to bring out his old long rifle and put a lead ball between Duke's shoulders. "Why, that slop-eatin' egg-suckin', lard-assed bastard. Now why in the hell'd he have to go and do a thing like that for? Better pick the little feller up and bring him to the house, Johnny. Looks like you got yourself a baby to take care of."

Johnny's eyes shone with excitement. He leaped into the air like a colt and took off running down the trail.

3

Colter stirred uneasily. Arrows of pain from the wound in his shoulder spread in a dozen directions at once, and his eyes ached deep within their sockets. Not yet able to open them, he was aware of the distant murmur of voices while his mind struggled to gain full consciousness. His swollen tongue explored his partially opened lips and found them flaked and parched. The air was pressing and hot and strong with the smell of stale sweat and the rank odor of sheep mixed with the pungent aroma of dried garlic and chili peppers. He heard the sharp "Hah!" of a rider whipping his mount into a fast start. It was followed a few moments later by the crack of a pistol shot and the heavy thumping of boots on a rough wood floor. He opened his eyes and reached for his gun. It was gone. The quick movement set off a pounding in his temples that drove the last flicker of consciousness from his mind and sent him into an abyss of darkness.

"He'll be comin' around directly, Johnny. Fetch a bowl of soup from the stove and bring it along."

Amos' voice from the other room knocked the burr from the rough edges of Colter's consciousness. He opened his eyes. He was no longer on a straw pallet. The bed on which he lay had a rough-hewn frame and rawhide webbing and a mattress of cotton ticking stuffed with feathers. The room was small and sparsely furnished. On one of the adobe walls was a pictur

General Ulysses S. Grant carefully cut from a news-paper. A small window took up part of the opposite wall. It was big enough, Colter noted, for a man to crawl through. A nightstand next to the bed held a family Bible and an oval-shaped tintype in a gilt-edged frame. In it Colter could see a barrel-chested, bearded man standing next to a dark-haired woman. In front of her and holding on to one of the man's fingers stood a blond bright-looking boy of about three. On both sides of the nightstand, clothing hung from wooden pegs driven into the walls. The ceiling was made of dried saguaro ribs packed tightly together and bound with rawhide strips. The cracks had been filled in with adobe mud.

A shaggy-haired man entered the room through the door on Colter's right. He was the same man from the photograph, but his hair was now gray and his beard no longer trimmed. He wore no gun and his friendly manner was that of a man greeting a guest.

"Glad to see you're comin' along, Mr. Haines. Thought we'd lose you there for a spell."

Colter studied Amos' weathered face. The crow-foot wrinkles at the corners of the eyes were generally in-dications that a man spent a good deal of time grinning or laughing. They were different than the kind gun-slingers and backshooters developed. Those kind were tension lines etched into the faces of men who lived—and died—by the gun, lines that crowded happiness out of their faces. Amos had none of these.

"I'm not one to forget a man's face, mister," Colter said, "but—"

Amos laughed, interrupting him. "You don't look like you'd forget much of anything, once you saw it. No, you don't know me, Mr. Haines, and I don't know you neither. I dug through your saddlebags last night to see if I could find out who it was we brung in, and I found a telegram with your name writ on it. I'm

Amos Carson, and me and my boy, Johnny, found you in a dry wash a couple of miles from here. A feller'd blowed a hole in you with a buffalo gun.''

"I know," Colter said.

Amos laughed again. "I guess that did sound a mite dumb, me tellin' you you'd been shot. A man gits kinda rusty with nobody to talk to out here that makes sense . . . I mean . . . Well, there's just me and Johnny."

Johnny stepped through the door carrying a bowl of hot soup. "I . . . I brung it, Pa."

"Yes, you did, Johnny. Did a good job too. Didn't spill 'ary a drop. Set it on the nightstand now, nice and careful like." Amos removed the Bible and stepped out of his son's road.

Johnny carried the bowl in, staring at the soup with intense concentration.

Colter studied Johnny's face. He noticed the expression in the eyes, the slack jaw, and the gangling uncoordinated walk. Amos' remark about nobody to talk to now had more meaning to him. There was only a faint resemblance of Johnny's face to that of the bright-eyed boy in the photograph. As Johnny set the bowl down and turned toward Amos, Colter could see the crescent-shaped scar that ran across the base of the skull.

"I done it, Pa. I . . , I brung the soup."

Amos smiled gently. "You did fine, son. Now you go set the coffee on. Maybe Mr. Haines would like a cup when he finishes eatin'."

"Yeah," Johnny said, "a cup."

Amos waited till Johnny had gone, then turned once again to Colter. He started to say something about Johnny, a brief explanation, but from the expression on Colter's face, he knew it wasn't necessary.

Colter spoke. "About that man that shot me with

the buffalo gun. You didn't happen to get a good look at him, did you?''

''Yeah, I seen the sidewinder. A real hard case too. Calls hisself Yeager. He wears one of them big Mexican sombreras. He was in such an all-fired hurry he dropped his rifle 'fore he left. Damnedest thing ever I saw too. It's got a coffee grinder in the stock.''

Colter's eyes narrowed. ''I'd like to see it.''

Amos went out of the room and returned with the rifle.

Colter stared at it for a while. ''It's not a buffalo gun, it's a Sharp's carbine. They used to call 'em coffee mills during the war. They figured the grinder would make it a little easier for the soldier to live off the land, grind his own corn, grain, or coffee. You don't see many of 'em anymore.''

Amos studied Colter's face. ''You look like you know somethin'. A man that wears one of them sugar-loafs and carries a gun like this 'un shouldn't be hard to find. You know him?''

Colter smiled wryly. ''Yeah, I know him. I put some lead in him a few years back when Jack and I punched cows for Charley Goodnight up in Colorado. I caught him and two of his pardners rustlin' some stock. He never saw Jack, though. Jack had ridden on ahead to get clearance from some homesteaders so we could cross their land. I don't know how he could have connected the two of us.''

''Maybe it wasn't revenge that got Jack shot,'' Amos added. ''Maybe . . . Well, maybe it was somethin' else.''

''Meanin' what?''

''Maybe nothin' at all, but . . . Well, yore brother ain't the only one's been shot around here. They's been a passel of killin's lately.''

''Are they tied in together?''

''Some of us think so.''

"Jack was pretty handy with a gun," Colter said. "I don't think many around could beat him."

"Bein' a fast draw don't stop a bullet in the back," Amos countered.

"You mean he was murdered?"

"I shore as hell do. I was in town when they brung him in."

Colter swallowed dryly. "Did you know Jack very well?" he asked after a moment.

"Didn't know him at all 'cept by sight, and the last time I seen him, he had a hole in his back," Amos said. "Somebody bushwhacked him like they tried to do to you."

Colter looked away. President Grant's picture caught his eyes once more and opened a flood of memories. When he was twenty-one, Colter had fought with Grant's army at the battle of Shiloh near the Tennessee-Mississippi border. Jack, barely seventeen at the time, joined him, and together they fought out the rest of the war under Grant's command. They were still serving with the general exactly three years later at Appomattox when Grant accepted Lee's surrender.

Jack was wild in those days—a little too foolhardy for his own sake—but he was a good soldier. He had always been a little too wild, and Colter wondered if that weakness in Jack's character had been responsible for the situation that had led to his death. He turned back to face Amos again. "People don't hold to back-shootin' where I come from. Don't they have any law in Charleston?"

"Yeah," Amos answered, "such as it is."

"That means the sheriff's either a drunk, or a coward, or somebody's hired hand. Which is it?"

"Bill Thompson ain't known for bein' much of a drinker, and I wouldn't exactly call the man a coward."

"Then who does he work for?" Colter asked. He

studied Amos' face for any sign that he had an ax to grind, something that might cause him to give false information.

"John Kittleman owns most of this country, but that's a long story, and you ain't et for a while." He nodded toward the hot soup. "You'd better eat that 'fore it cools off. You're gonna be here for quite a spell, so we'll have a lot of time for chewin' the fat."

"The soup can wait," Colter said, but he knew he wasn't up to it. His stomach was empty and growling, and the pulsating pains in his shoulder were stabbing deeper and deeper with each throb. The soup smelled good, too good to put off. He glanced at Amos' face. It was friendly but stern. Colter knew the man was right. He needed food to keep his strength up. "Well," he admitted, "maybe a spoon or two."

He ate as much of the soup as he could before the pain in his shoulder pushed the desire for food out of his system. He slumped back against the pillow and dropped almost immediately into a fitful sleep.

Unanswered questions pushed through the muddled regions of his subconscious, passed the jumbled bits and pieces of the shooting encounter he'd had with Yeager, and kept floating by like banners painted on the canvas covers of medicine-show wagons. Several Chiricahuas bound his feet with buckskin thongs and hoisted them high in the air to let him hang head down over a slow fire. The pain was excruciating. Suddenly the Chiricahaus became bushwhackers and the man they were shooting was Jack. Colter shouted, tried to get them to stop, but no one seemed to care, no one listened. Then he was in the fire again and the Chirica-huas were burning his shoulder with hot brands. The burning stopped abruptly and a sudden coolness framed his face.

He awoke to find water trickling down his cheeks as Amos placed a wet towel across his forehead.

The old man grinned. "I thank you must have had Lucifer hisself a-doggin' yore tail."

"Did I talk much?"

"No, but you done a hell of a lot of yellin'."

"How long have I slept?"

"Well, I wouldn't exactly call it sleep, but you've been in and out for two days now."

Colter pulled the towel from his head and sat up. The room spun crazily for a moment, then stopped.

Amos spoke. "Thank you need some grub. You're weaker'n a baby buffalo fart." He stepped to the door and called, "Johnny, fetch a bowl of them beans yonder and bring a couple of drop biscuits too."

Johnny sat on the floor flicking some fresh dung from his boots with a knife. He showed no sign of having heard his father's voice.

"Johnny," Amos thundered, "will you look at what you're a-doin' to the floor! Git out yonder and scrape the goose hockey off them boots, then clean this mess up. Good Lord a'mighty!"

He walked to the stove and filled a tin plate with beans. Then, stacking two biscuits at the edge of the plate, he poured a cup of coffee and carried the food in to Colter.

"Now," he said as Colter began to eat, "you asked about John Kittleman. He's a hard man, a strange man. He came into the territory, far as I know, back in the early '50s. I been here since '61, and he was here 'fore I come. He started ranchin' on a little spread south of town. Then, after the war, he drove a herd of longhorns over from Texas, and that started him to thankin' big. He got to grabbin' land ever'where he could reach and some places he couldn't. The small ranchers around here feel he ain't too bad a feller. That is the ones that don't control a good water supply. He lets them send their cattle along with his at roundup time. He handles all their stock till they're sold—for a fee, of course. The townspeople like Kittleman too. His spread is so big, he brings in a lot of business for 'em. Now the dirt farmers and the lobos like me, why we wouldn't give you a plug nickel for the son of a bitch.

"You take this place, for instance. It ain't big enough to cuss a cat in without gittin' hair in your teeth, but Kittleman's been tryin' to run me off it for ten years now."

"Why does he want it so bad?"

"Water! I got a good sweetwater spring up beyond them rocks the other side of the corral. Water in this country's like gold. Them that's got lots of it are rich. Kittleman wants ever' drop in the territory if he can git it."

"Has he ever done anything that's really illegal? Something you could get the territorial governor to look into?"

"I've heered lots of rumors, but I don't know nothin' I ain't already said," Amos answered.

"They's two horses a-comin', Pa!" Johnny shouted. "Two horses."

Amos walked to the front door to check. Then he returned to the bedroom.

"It's an old friend of mine," he said. "Sheridan Mason. He's the editor of the local newspaper. He's bringing the doc with him. Mason's been here since Heck was a pup. He ought to be able to tell you somethin' about Kittleman. He's kind of an odd old goat. Crusty as hell. Sometimes he can talk the steam out of a donkey engine. On other occasions he puckers up tighter than an old biddy's rear at egg-layin' time. I'd wait till the doc leaves 'fore I asked anything, though. I don't know too much about him."

Colter could hear Mason and the doc greeting Johnny as they rode into the yard. Amos walked out to meet the two men, and after a minute or two of discussion he returned with the others.

Sheridan Mason was short and wiry, a nearly bald man in his early sixties. His hawklike features housed a pair of deep-set blue eyes that immediately began a close study of Colter's face as the doc moved to the bedside.

Doc Thatcher was a pudgy bespectacled man with the detached businesslike manner of the frontier doctor who'd tended to all types of illnesses and accidents in both man and beast. He squinted curiously as he inspected Colter's wound.

"Whoever done this wanted to make damned sure you didn't walk off," he said, swabbing the wound and putting a clean bandage on it. "I don't suppose it'd do any good to ask you who did it."

"I don't suppose," Colter answered.

"I came out here expectin' to find Amos with his leg near chopped off," Doc Thatcher said, hoping for some enlightenment.

Amos snorted. "Hell, I'd have bled to death two days ago if I had to depend on you. What'd that buckskin of yores do, bust a leg?"

"I was unable to get out here sooner," Doc answered gruffly. "I was detained."

"For two days?" Amos bellowed. "What the hell were you a-doin', takin' care of a cholera epidemic?"

"I . . . I couldn't get away. I'm sorry," Doc said haltingly. "I had to remain at Mr. Kittleman's ranch. There was a . . . an emergency."

"Somebody git a little lead poisonin'?" Amos asked.

Doc Thatcher's eyes widened momentarily, then narrowed again as the connection between the gunshot wounds of two men in different locales became apparent.

It was equally apparent to Amos that Doc had analyzed the situation accurately. "Was I you, Doc, I don't thank I'd tell 'ary a word about this when I got back to town. Just say my leg's doin' right well, and let it go at that. Ain't nobody knows this boy's here 'cept us three.'' He chuckled, and though it sounded light and humorous, there was an ominous ring to it. ''I'd just naturally hate to have some of Kittleman's boys payin' me a visit 'cause then I might thank you told 'em 'bout my friend here.''

''I never discuss my patients with anyone.''

''That's good,'' Amos said. ''That's right good.''

Doc Thatcher replaced the bandage Amos had put on Colter's wound. Then, picking up his bag, he smiled nervously and left.

Amos followed him to the door, and after the doc left and was safely down the road a ways, he returned to the bedroom, where Sheridan Mason and Colter were involved in conversation.

''I'd like to know everything about John Kittleman you can tell me,'' Colter was saying as Amos entered.

''I told him ever'thing I know,'' Amos added, ''which ain't a hell of a lot.''

''Now that's the gospel truth,'' Mason said, grinning. ''He doesn't often admit it, but the truth is he doesn't know a hell of a lot about anything.''

''Hell!'' Amos thundered. ''If brains was a physic you couldn't give a sick sparrow the trots.''

Mason, still grinning, winked at Colter. ''He's all horns and rattles, ain't he?'' Then he took a deep breath and exhaled noisily. Rubbing his index finger across his bottom lip from one side to the other while he gathered his thoughts, he finished the action by sweeping the finger downward to join his thumb at the base of his chin, where he pinched the loose skin into a roll and held it for a few seconds as he began.

''Kittleman was a likable sort when he first came to the territory, but then he changed quite a bit after his son's death.''

"Son?" Amos asked. "I didn't know that reptile could breed."

"He had a little brown-haired tyke about four years old when he first got here. The boy used to come in town with his mother every week or so. She'd bring him in just so he could play with the kids in town. Then Kittleman began buying up smaller ranches and they moved to a spread quite a ways out. I never saw the boy or his mother much after that. I guess about five years passed before the boy died in that fire."

"Did the ranch burn?" Amos asked.

"No, it was a homesteader's cabin the boy died in. A fella named Fernley owned it. He had a wife and five kids, and they loved the place. Then the Apaches came by one night and burned it and shot Fernley and his wife. The Fernley kids and Kittleman's boy never made it out of the cabin. It killed every one of them."

"You say it happened at night?" Colter asked.

"Yes. A rancher that lived nearby passed the cabin in the early evening. It was burned down when he came by next morning."

"And they're sure it was Apaches?"

"Yes," Mason replied, his voice tinged with curiosity. "That's what the sheriff told us. Said he found hoof prints and moccasin tracks all around the house."

"Who owns the place now?" Colter asked.

"Kittleman," Mason answered.

"Didn't anyone think it was kind of strange that they blamed it on the Apaches?"

Mason stared at Colter. "Why should they? The Indians burned a lot of places down in those days."

"But most people know that Apaches don't attack after dark," Colter said. "That includes Chiricahuas, the Jicarillas, the Mescaleros, and all the rest of 'em that I know of. They're superstitious about going out at night. They're afraid they'll hear an owl. They believe it's the ghost of a dead relative or a bad human being. Its hoot is a warning of trouble to come. And they're not foolish enough to leave tracks all over the place either.''

"There was some talk at the time that Kittleman had done it to drive Fernley out," Mason said, "but those of us that know the man realize he couldn't have done a thing like that, especially with his own son in the house. He idolized that little boy."

"If Colter here is right about them 'Paches, then who in the hell else could have done it?" Amos asked.

"I don't know," Mason snapped. "All I know is what the sheriff said, and he told me that the Apaches did it."

"Well, he told a damn lie," Amos said. "That's the way I see it."

"You can't be sure," Mason retorted. "Could be a simple mistake, you know."

"Could be that you wouldn't fart if you et beans either," Amos growled, "but iffen you did, I shore as hell wouldn't sit next to you in church."

"There's little danger in that," Mason observed dryly.

Colter was deep in thought and paid no attention to the two of them. "I think," he said after a pause, "that the sheriff would be the best man for me to talk to first. He's got some information I think he ought to share with me."

"Sheriff Thompson may not see it your way," Mason said, shifting uncomfortably. "He probably won't say a thing I haven't already told you about."

"Then, by God, we'll stamp it out of him," Amos muttered.

"We?" both Colter and Mason asked in unison.

Amos looked to Colter as though he'd just been caught pinching the schoolmarm's bottom. "Well . . . I mean . . . if you need any help, that is."

"Thanks," Colter said, smiling faintly, "but this is

my problem—not yours. I do appreciate the offer, though.''

''I ain't so sure the trouble we've all had in this territory ain't tied in to one big problem,'' Amos countered, ''and that can be spelled out in a single word—Kittleman.''

''If you're right, we'll join forces,'' Colter said, ''and I'll find that out as soon as I'm able to travel.''

''That ain't gonna be for a while, so just relax and git some rest. Come on, Sheridan. Let's move out of here and let the boy sleep. We've done talked too much as it is.''

Colter was aware of the throbbing pain again as the two men left the room. He wished his shoulder was well enough to travel. He'd see the sheriff first and then pay a visit to Yeager. There was a score to settle with that one—maybe a double one if he'd been the killer that bushwhacked Jack. It shouldn't take too long to find that out once he got back on his feet again. He shifted painfully and fell into another fitful sleep. The questions and their answers would have to wait . . . for a while.

4

Colter stood in the doorway of Amos' cabin and studied the scrub hills beyond the front yard. His eyes scanned the area from the horizon to the back side of the corral. It was quiet and the air already warm with the promise of heat to come. A buzzard wheeled lazily in the distance, looking for the remnants of a kill. Nothing moved on the land except a small herd of sheep. Colter wondered how long it would remain quiet. He knew that John Kittleman would not have been satisfied with Duke's report. They'd come again. He didn't want the old man involved any more than he already was. He also figured that Kittleman would call off the hunt as soon as Colter showed up in town. That's where he was aiming to go this morning.

Soreness clung to his shoulder. Two weeks of lying around and a week of massaging and working the muscles had helped to limber it up, but there was still a tightness that he knew would remain for days.

He checked the hills again and stepped outside.

Ducking under the top rail of the corral, he climbed in and took the gelding's reins off the gate post where Johnny had put them. His big roan, eager to leave the confinement of the small enclosure, trotted over and nudged his arm. Colter smiled and slipped the bit over its tongue. "I reckon you're ready to light out too, huh?" The roan whinnied noisily as Colter dropped the bridle behind its ears.

Johnny looked up from a shady spot near the kitchen window where he sat trying to teach the lamb to jump over a stick. "You goin' far away." He said it as a statement rather than a question.

Colter smiled. "Not too far. I'm only ridin' to Charleston. I'll be comin' back to see you."

Johnny grinned. "Yeah . . . Charleston." He looked down at the lamb and tapped its chest with the stick. The lamb, unable to comprehend, refused to jump. "Yore a nice little feller," he said, rubbing the animal's ears, "but hod damn . . . yore shore a dumb one." Then he laughed as though he'd just told a joke. "Yore a-goin'," he said to Colter again.

"Got work to do, Johnny," Colter answered. "Got to go talk to the sheriff and then ride out and see Mr. Kittleman."

"He's a bad man. He don't like me neither. Killed our sheep."

"Who did, the sheriff or Mr. Kittleman?"

"Don't like me at all. Don't like sheep neither," Johnny answered.

Amos stepped out and threw a basin of dishwater on the small garden patch he'd planted near the kitchen door. "He means that lard-assed foreman of Kittleman's, the one I told you about named Duke. He's a mean son of a bitch. He'd just as soon backshoot you as say hello. You'd best keep a sharp eye on that one."

Colter swung the saddle up on the blanket he'd placed on the roan's back. "Thanks," he said. "I will." He raised the left stirrup up and dropped it over the saddle horn so he could hook up the cinch. The movement brought a grimace of pain to his face.

"I told you to wait a couple more days," Amos grumbled. "As weak as that shoulder of yourn is, why, you couldn't pull a sick widder off a thunder mug."

Colter grinned and tightened the cinch. "Don't figure I'll have to, but if I need somebody to do it for me, I know just the man to see.''

"I mean it," Amos snapped. "Right now you ain't worth a pound of sour owl manure in a fight, and you know it. I figure you ought to let me go with you. Then I could pertect yore back from the likes of Duke and the rest of them crap-eatin' sidewinders.''

Colter dropped the stirrup and turned to face Amos. It was the first time anyone outside of his brother Jack had made that kind of offer, and it touched him. He felt a stirring inside. "Amos," he said, placing his hand on the old man's shoulder, "I'm much obliged for the offer, but I don't think I'll need it.''

Amos snorted. "Well, me and Johnny's a-comin' to town tomorrow, so we'll just see how yore a-doin'. Things is gittin' out of hand in that town, Colter, and I figure it's more trouble than one man can handle. Arizona Territory is growin' too durned fast to suit me.''

Colter grinned and swung into the saddle. "A man's got to do what he thinks best. I'm goin' out to my brother's place first. Then I'll head for town and talk to a few people. I'll get a room at the hotel. You can contact me there if you find out anything I should know.''

"Them beds is so loaded with graybacks, they'll pack you out on their shoulders. Yore welcome to stay here if you like," Amos said.

Colter smiled. "I've never liked lice, but I can handle it.''

Johnny came up carrying the lamb and handed Colter a small blue rock.

Colter examined it. "What's this, Johnny?"

"It's a rock," Johnny answered.

Amos looked surprised. "He's a givin' it to you." Then he took off his hat and scratched his head. "He's had that rock for five years. Never thought he'd give that to nobody.''

Colter put it in his shirt pocket. "Thanks, Johnny. That's a real nice rock.'' He nodded to Amos, then headed the gelding down the road.

"Is he a-comin' back, Pa?'' Johnny asked.

Amos placed his arm around Johnny's shoulders. ''I hope so, son. I shore do hope so.''

Following Amos' directions, Colter continued along a ridge of rock until he came to a saddle, then angled down the gentle slope to the left till he reached a broad wash along which many mesquite trees grew. He rode beside the meandering dry streambed for several miles before reaching the trail that Amos had mentioned. Another half-hour brought him to a small butte that gave a commanding view of the desert for several miles in all directions. Colter tugged on the reins slightly and the gelding stopped. He rolled a cigarette while he studied the area below him. A small stand of cottonwoods provided shade and signified the presence of water. This was the spot Amos had described as Jack's ranch, but Colter could see no house. Then, easing the roan forward a dozen yards, he stopped again and stood in the stirrups. Behind the cottonwoods and partially hidden by a mesquite stood the fire-gutted shell of an adobe house.

Colter eased the reins and leaned forward. The roan instantly moved down the sloping face of the butte, as sure of its footing as a desert bighorn. Upon reaching the floor, it quickened its pace to an easy lope.

Colter dismounted in front of the cabin, then stepped inside the blackened doorway. It had been a small but well-built house. The walls were solid and thick, and since the fire seemed to have been recent and no rain had fallen afterward, they showed no sign of erosion. It was basically a one-room cabin with a wall extending part of the way across one end to form a small bedroom. A man could put a new roof on it and some window and door frames to replace the burned ones, and he'd have a good place to live, cool in the summer and snug in the winter. Colter wondered why it had been burned. There was nothing left among the ashes on the dirt floor to give any indication. As he was leaving, he noticed a handful of small green rocks in what had been the entrance to the bedroom. There were a couple of blue ones among them similar to the one Johnny had given him. He took one of each color and put them in his pocket. He was sure Johnny would like to have them. After watering the gelding in the small stream that ran between the cottonwoods, he mounted up and headed for Charleston.

The streets were quiet and nearly empty in the mid-morning heat as Colter rode in. A wagon stood in front of Alcott's General Store. The team dozed and occasionally swished their tails to ward off the biting horse-flies that bit, then circled to land and bite again. Three old-timers sat in front of the Imperial Hotel, leaning their chairs back against the unpainted clapboard siding, talking in low tones and staring in frank open-mouthed curiosity as Colter dismounted and dropped his reins over the hitching rail.

"Howdy," he said, crossing the boardwalk to the hotel entrance. The old-timers just continued staring with mouths ajar. "Think the rain'll hurt the rhu-barb?" Colter ventured.

A wry smile crossed the face of one of the ancient trio. "Not if you cover it with cow chips," the old man said. Then the three of them cackled in unison.

"You sound like a man who really knows his chips," Colter replied.

"He's a inspector," another of the trio said. That set them off into another round of laughter.

Colter stepped inside the hotel. ''You got a room?''

''Yes, sir,'' the clerk answered, a broad smile crossing his face. ''It's a dollar with and seventy-five cents without.''

''Without what? Graybacks?''

The smile turned downward and settled into the permanent creases of pessimism that lined the clerk's face. ''I was talking about a bath,'' he grumbled. ''It's two bits extra for heating and carrying the water.''

''I may take a bath in the morning,'' Colter said, handing the clerk a dollar. ''It depends on how dirty I get tonight.'' He signed the register and then closed it.

The clerk shoved a key over the countertop and dropped the dollar in his money box. His sour expression remained unchanged. ''Number ten. Upstairs to the rear.'' He opened the register and carefully smoothed out the pages as though Colter had wrinkled them.

Colter put the key in his pocket and turned toward the door. The old-timers were peering through the front window, still watching him. He ambled over to the door. ''I'll bet you three want me to hold stakes on a footrace you're about to have, right?''

The three men settled back in their chairs, cackling as Colter stepped past them. He took the gelding's reins and led him down the street.

Sheridan Mason stood in the doorway of his newspaper office watching Colter cross the street toward him. He was amazed at how light on his feet Colter appeared. His stride was smooth and relaxed. It reminded Sheridan of a big cat, powerful but lithe.

Colter gave the reins a flip around the hitching rail and glanced up at Sheridan. ''You know a gal named Cynthia Dobbs?''

Sheridan grinned. ''Sure do. She's that pretty little blond thing who works down at Alcott's store. She used to be quite sweet on your brother. You figure on talkin' to her?''

"Can't do any harm. You have any idea how Jack's house burned down?''

Sheridan's eyebrows raised. "Didn't even know it had happened. He never said anything about it."

"Just curious," Colter said. He turned and looked at the saloon across the street. "How's that place for gettin' a drink?''

Sheridan grinned. "Bascomb's? I like it better than the Roundup two blocks down. There's usually more fighting at Bascomb's, and that's news for my paper. I usually don't even have to walk across the street to see a shootin'. Seems like gunmen enjoy the crowd that watches when they plug somebody in the street. The liquor, though, is better down at the Roundup."

"I'll try Bascomb's," Colter said, turning toward the saloon.

"If it wasn't so early, I'd join you," Sheridan commented.

Colter walked across the street without answering.

"If you want a little friendly advice, I'd say take it easy and don't start anything. Getting in trouble won't bring Jack back again," Sheridan yelled.

Colter glanced over his shoulder and nodded, acknowledging Sheridan's comment. Then he pushed through the batwing doors that hung slightly askew at the entrance. They groaned and creaked their protest at his passage as they swung alternately in and out. He crossed to the bar and waited till the barkeep had finished wiping an imaginary speck of dust from the polished mahogany before he spoke. "I'd like a drink."

"What'll you have, whiskey?"

"What have you got?"

"Whiskey."

Colter shrugged

The bartender reached under the counter and brought out a bottle and a glass. "Ain't seen you before, have I?"

"If you had, you'd know it," Colter answered. "Haven't seen a bartender yet that didn't have a memory like an elephant."

The bartender grinned. "I guess you got somethin' there. Where'd you say you was from?"

"I didn't," Colter said, taking down half a shot of whiskey. His face puckered like he'd just sucked a lemon. "Whew!" he exclaimed, looking at the glass. "You sure you ain't got a panther under there? This stuff tastes like. . ."

"Yeah, I know," the bartender said, picking up the bottle and wiping away the ring it had left on the bar. "That drummer told me it was the best drinkin' liquor this side of the Mississippi. He switched samples on me's what he done. The stuff I tried was purty good."

"Well, this sure as hell ain't it," Colter said, downing the rest of the shot. He turned to check the card-players in the rear of the room. Now that his eyes were accustomed to the gloom of the saloon's interior, he could easily see the four men seated at the table. One of them wore a sugarloaf sombrero. Turning back to the bartender, he said, "I believe I've seen that big fella with the sombrero before. Doesn't he walk with a limp?"

"He does now," the bartender answered. "Said a bronc throwed him."

"Yeah, he's the fella all right," Colter said. "I think I've got somethin' that belongs to him. Be right back." He went out through the doors to the other side of the street.

Sheridan Mason, still standing in front of his office, scowled as Colter unstrapped the Sharps carbine from the outside of his rifle scabbard. "You're not thinking of doing anything foolish with that, are you?"

Colter grinned and pointed to the Winchester inside the scabbard. "That one's mine. I'm just returning this to the gent that dropped it outside of town." He turned and headed back toward the saloon.

Sheridan stood watching for several moments before the impact of Colter's words struck him. Then, realizing there was going to be some gunplay, he hurried across the street and entered Bascomb's before the batwings had completed their second creak. He waved the bartender into silence and stood at the far end of the bar.

Colter walked up to the card table and put the tip end of the Sharps' barrel against the broad back of the man in the sugarloaf sombrero. The hum of talk suddenly stopped. The faces of the other three players seemed to Colter to blanch a shade or two. One of them swallowed awkwardly. The man in the sugarloaf sat with both hands on top of the table.

"I found this old coffee mill out on the trail and somebody said it belonged to a fella named Yeager. That you?" Colter asked. He grinned.

The three players watching him exhaled noisily almost in unison. Colter stepped back as Yeager got to his feet. The big man spun angrily and faced him.

"If this is your idea of a joke, you got one hell of a sense of humor," Yeager growled. "A stunt like that could get a man killed real quick."

Colter grinned again. "Is this rifle yours?"

"Yeah," Yeager snarled. "It's mine."

With one savage thrust, Colter shoved the barrel deep into Yeager's gut. "Always like to return a man's property." His voice was cold.

The three players, now realizing something more serious than a joke was about to take place, scattered in three different directions.

Colter leaned the Sharps against an empty table and waited patiently for the gasping Yeager to catch a full breath of air. When Yeager finally quit wheezing and gulping, he stared at Colter, his eyes flashing with hate.

Colter spoke, his voice low, his words chipped. "You dropped this after you tried to bushwhack me. Maybe you'd like to finish the job."

Yeager was disturbed by Colter's coolness. Colter's face seemed vaguely familiar, but Yeager couldn't place him. He remembered shooting a man out in the arroyo, but he hadn't gotten a close look at him. Colter's holster wasn't tied low like a gunslinger's would be. He looked like an ordinary cowhand to Yeager, yet his manner was . . . different.

Yeager glanced at his cardplaying friends, now standing safely out of range. They were staring and silent. His reputation was riding on this one. He'd been called out. He didn't like that. A man always had the advantage when he did the calling. It gave him a slight edge over his opponent, an edge of confidence. You never called a man down unless you were certain you could beat him.

Yeager glanced at Colter again. The man was just standing there, relaxed. Yeager straightened up. He knew all the hired guns around and this one sure wasn't one of them. Just a thirty-dollar-a-month cowhand lookin' for trouble, he thought. Then it struck him. Cowhand! This was the same man that had shot him up in Colorado and killed Shorty and Pete too just over a little rustlin'. He grinned. Nothin' to worry about. He could take this one and a dozen like him.

"Yeah," Yeager said finally. "I think I will finish the job. Seems to me I owe you for blowin' a hole in my side up Colorado way." He reached for his gun and felt confident as it began to clear leather a fraction of a second before Colter made his move. He didn't notice that the big Colt .45 had magically appeared in Colter's hand until he simultaneously heard the explosion of the shot and felt a hammer blow against his chest an inch and a half below and slightly to the left of the sternum. The 255-grain soft lead bullet broke through a rib and sent bits of bone fragment ripping into the heart, where they lodged in the floundering muscle like the quills of a tiny porcupine. The bullet tore a portion of the organ away and continued on its way, narrowly missing the vertebra on its exit. The last sound Yeager might have heard, a curious plinking noise as the nearly spent slug ricocheted off the stove pipe at the rear of the room, came an instant before the back of his head struck the floor.

Colter stood for several moments staring at Yeager's body. Just as he was about to holster his gun, the sheriff burst through the door followed by one of the original cardplayers.

"Hold it right there, cowboy. I'll take that gun."

Colter turned to face the sheriff. "He drew first," he said.

"That's right, Sheriff," the bartender said. "Yeager drew first, but this feller was about ten times faster. Fastest thing I ever saw."

"I'll take it anyway. We don't like gunslingers around here." the sheriff said, his arm still outstretched.

"Wait a minute, Bill." The voice was Sheridan's. "Yeager tried to ambush this fella on the way to town a few weeks ago. He admitted it just before he was shot. This is Colter Haines, Jack's brother. He's no gunslinger. He's here to take care of some family business."

The sheriff holstered his gun reluctantly. "Well, I hope you ain't no troublemaker like your brother was. You take my advice and get your business cleared up fast. Mr. Kittleman ain't gonna like hearin' you shot one of his boys." Turning to one of the cardplayers, he ordered, "Go get old man Haggerty and tell him he's got a customer. Remember what I said, Haines," he added, turning once more to Colter. "Get your business finished and clear out." He walked out, followed by the man who was going to get the undertaker.

Colter looked at Sheridan. "Thanks. Looks like everyone hands out advice in this town."

Sheridan smiled. "I've got some more for you. Don't ever drink any bar whiskey this bandit behind the counter hands out. That stuff would eat through a sheet of lead. Get out the private stock, Bascomb, and I'll buy us all a drink."

The bartender looked up and down the bar quickly. "Shh!" he cautioned. "That's only for my friends. If ever'body found out about it, I'd never get rid of this stuff, and I got ten barrels left."

"You could always sell it for sheep dip," Colter said.

Their conversation stopped as the undertaker and his assistant entered and removed Yeager's body. When they'd gone, Sheridan filled three glasses and handed one to Colter and one to the bartender. He took a sip and studied Colter's face. "Well, there's one thing I can say. You sure don't waste any time letting people know you're in town."

The bartender shook his head. "I believe that's about the slickest piece of gunplay I've ever seen." He gulped the whiskey down in one swallow. "When Bill Thompson said that Mr. Kittleman's gonna be awful mad when he finds out you killed one of his best guns, he sure wasn't lyin'. He'll be fit to be tied." He glanced over at the grandfather clock that stood against the wall behind the bar. "I calculate he'll either send Duke and some of his boys, or he'll bring 'em in himself, and it won't take him more than an hour either way."

Colter nodded. "Looks like he'll save me some ri-din' around. That's good."

"I wouldn't bet on it," Sheridan added. "I sure wouldn't bet on it."

Colter drained his glass and set it on the bar. "If I've got an hour to kill, I might as well talk to a few people. See you later," he said to Sheridan, "and thanks for the drink."

He stepped through the batwings again and headed toward Alcott's store. He wished now he'd asked Yeager whether or not he'd shot Jack. Chances are he wouldn't have admitted it, but a hired gun like Yeager often took to bragging. Maybe Cynthia Dobbs could shed some light on what happened. He had at least an hour to find out.

5

Alcott's General Store contained everything farmers and ranchers needed to keep a place going. There were kegs of nails next to sacks of flour and bolts of linen stacked near boxes of bullets. The air was thick with the odor of onions, chilis, leather, and cheese.

Colter stood in the open doorway watching Cynthia Dobbs help a farmer's wife make a choice of colors from some bolts of calico cloth. When she'd finished and the woman had gone, he stepped inside and walked to the counter.

"May I help you?" she said, tilting her head slightly as she noticed his intense gaze.

"Maybe," Colter answered. "I'm Colter Haines, Jack's brother."

Cynthia studied Colter's face. "I was beginning to think the telegram I sent you must not have arrived at all. Either that or you'd moved to someplace else."

"I was delayed getting here," Colter answered.

"Yes," Cynthia added, "I heard that some of the Apaches were off the reservation again."

"It wasn't Apaches that caused the delay," Colter corrected. Then, noticing Cynthia's perplexed expression, he continued, "Somebody was waiting for me outside of town. Who did you tell about sending me that telegram?"

"I didn't tell anybody. The telegraph agent was the

only one who could possibly have known that I sent a message.''

"I'll talk to him later," Colter said. "Right now I'd like some information about what happened to my brother.''

"You know, if you hadn't told me you were Jack's brother, I'd never have known it. There's not even the slightest resemblance between you two.''

Colter studied Cynthia before he spoke. Her long blond hair, pulled back and tied with a blue ribbon, gleamed like burnished gold. High cheekbones and full sensuous lips, a slightly turned-up nose, and large honey-brown eyes were all combined into one of the most beautiful faces Colter had ever seen. His gaze wandered down the soft throat and across the small but well-rounded breasts to the trim waist and stopped at the countertop. Suddenly realizing that he had been staring for some time, he glanced back at her face and noticed that it was slightly flushed. Knowing that he must have embarrassed her by the intensity of his gaze, he looked quickly away and placed his hand on a stack of new denim pants.

"We weren't really brothers," he said finally. "His folks adopted me when my own parents died of cholera. I was just a kid at the time. They gave me a new family, a new name, and a good start." He glanced back at Cynthia again. The tinge of redness had faded from her face and there was an expression of soft tenderness in her eyes.

"Hey, Hank!" A man burst through the door and hurried up to the stocky bespectacled Hank Alcott as he stepped out of the rear storeroom. "There was a shoot-out down at Bascomb's Saloon. They say Jack Haines' brother's in town and he's in a gunnin' mood.''

"Who'd he shoot?" Alcott asked.

"He killed one of Kittleman's boys. The one they

call Yeager. Sheriff said it was self-defense, but he didn't seem too happy about it.''

Alcott removed his apron and dropped it on the counter. "Let's go talk to him."

Colter turned so that only his back was visible as Alcott headed for the door.

"I'll be back in a little bit," Alcott called to Cynthia as he stepped out.

"Is that true?" she asked after they'd gone. "Did you kill Yeager?"

"He tried to bushwhack me several weeks ago. Blew a hole in my shoulder. That was the delay I told you about," he answered.

"Well, you've certainly stirred things up by tangling with one of Kittleman's bunch. You can expect him in town with half of his ranch hands before long. It might be wise to leave before he gets here."

Colter grinned. "Seems like everyone in Charleston wants me to leave." The grin disappeared. "I came to find out some answers. When I'm satisfied, I'll ride out. But it'll be because I *want* to. Not because somebody told me to."

Cynthia lowered her gaze. "I'm sorry. Of course you have a right to stay here. If the sheriff said it was self-defense, Kittleman can't do much about it."

"At least legally," Colter added.

Cynthia looked up. "He's a very aggressive man. He does exactly what he wants, and he usually gets what he goes after."

"I've seen his kind." Colter replied, "and they haven't worried me yet. Tell me about Jack."

"What would you like to know?" she asked.

"Everything you can remember. I understand you and Jack were . . . well . . . sort of sweet on each other."

"I . . . liked Jack very much when he first came to Charleston. He was kind and considerate . . . in the beginning. We even talked about getting married at one time. That's when he first bought the ranch. But then, he changed.''

"How did he change, and why?" Colter asked. He found it hard to believe that Jack would give up the idea of marrying Cynthia. She was the kind of woman, at least in looks, that any man dreamed about during those lonely hours riding herd, the kind a man wanted to share a blanket with whether the nights were chilly or filled with the perfumed fragrance of spring.

She flushed slightly as intuition and Colter's gaze told her what he was thinking. There was something about this big man that intrigued her, something that caused her breathing to become more rapid. She hadn't reacted that way to anyone before—not even Jack. She was pleased that her voice was controlled and showed no indication of her excitement when she spoke.

"I don't really know what the cause was. At first he wanted nothing more than to develop his ranch into a big spread with a herd large enough to make everyone take notice. The first winter he lost his breeding stock. Then he took to hanging around town here with an old drunken Indian named Chirtua. I told him I wouldn't see him any longer if he continued his drinking. He stopped, and right after that he began spending a lot of time out at John Kittleman's ranch.''

"Did he say why?" Colter asked.

"No, but he seemed to think his friendship, especially with Mrs. Kittleman, would open some doors for him.''

"You mean she was interested in him?"

"Oh, not romantically," Cynthia said, her eyes studying Colter's face. "She's old and rather sickly. I don't know what it was all about, but he must have explained it in that letter he wrote.''

"What letter?"

"He gave me a package and a letter addressed to

you the day before he died. He said if anything should happen to him, I was to mail the letter to you. He said you'd know what to do when you opened the box.''

''I didn't get a letter, just the telegram you sent.''

''I know,'' she replied. ''I can't find the letter or the box. I had them with me here at the store, but when we closed up, I couldn't find them. I don't know whether someone took them by mistake or what. Fortunately, I remembered your address from the envelope.''

''And you have no idea what was in either the letter or the box?''

''I don't make a habit of opening other people's mail. All I know is the box was sort of heavy, and the letter was quite thick.''

''And he was murdered right after he gave them to you. They must have been pretty important to somebody.''

''I'm sure the box and the letter must have been carried out by mistake and loaded on someone's wagon. They'll probably be returned when whoever has them comes back in town again. and your brother certainly wasn't murdered. He shot Walter Kramer, and Kramer shot him. It was just a plain old argument where they both lost their tempers.''

''Whose story was that, the sheriff's?'' Colter asked.

''Mrs. Kramer found both of them dead by the fence that separates their ranches. She said they'd quarreled earlier in the day. All the sheriff did was bring in their bodies. Kramer was killed with Jack's pistol, and Jack was shot with Kramer's rifle. There wasn't any murder involved. It was just a plain old argument followed by a shooting.''

''Jack would never draw on a man that wasn't carrying a handgun unless it was in self-defense.''

''Maybe that's what he did,'' she added.

''He was shot in the back,'' Colter said.

A thundering of horses' hooves in the street outside caught his attention. He counted seven riders as they passed. The man in the lead wore a tweed coat and rode an Appaloosa. Colter knew it was Kittleman without having to be told.

"It looks like the man has arrived," he commented. "Guess I'd better go talk to him."

"Colter!"

He turned.

"Be careful. He's a very powerful man in these parts. Everyone's on his side."

"Are you?" he asked.

"I don't take sides," she replied. "He's always been polite to me, so I have nothing against him." She smiled. "But then I wouldn't go out of my way to shake his hand either."

"I'll see you," Colter said.

As he stepped through the door, she followed to watch him cross the street. He seemed to exude power and confidence as he walked, yet there was a feline grace to his movements. She wanted so much to follow him, to be there when he met Kittleman. One man against seven—and that didn't include the sheriff and his deputy. Those were odds nobody wanted to face alone. And yet Colter seemed to look forward to it. No one had faced Kittleman before and won. Maybe now was the time, and maybe Colter Haines was the man.

6

Colter watched the crowd of men milling around on the boardwalk in front of Bascomb's Saloon. He recognized Hank Alcott, Sheriff Thompson, and the man he knew must be Kittleman. From Amos' description of Duke, the foreman on Kittleman's ranch, the burly-looking cowboy standing next to Alcott must be the man. They all moved inside the saloon to continue their talk.

As he crossed the street, Colter drew his .45 from its holster and replaced the bullet he'd used to kill Yeager. Then, after checking its action, he returned the Colt to its leather and eased it slightly upward, a movement that was more reflex than conscious thought. It was an action born of survival, one he'd learned that could give him a split-second edge over an enemy. He didn't figure Kittleman would try anything in town with so many people around, but from what Amos said, Duke was certainly capable of it. He briefly thought about stopping to get his horse in front of the newspaper office, but decided against it. There was already nearly a dozen at the hitching rail in front of Bascomb's. If gunplay did start, trying to reach his roan and mount it in a herd like that might prove to be too slow a move.

He hesitated a moment at the corner of Bascomb's window and checked the position of the crowd inside. Everyone stood at the bar, the sheriff and Kittleman in the center. The sheriff's back was toward the door. Duke stood behind Kittleman, and it was he who noticed Colter first. The murmur of voices stopped as Colter entered.

Kittleman spoke. "The sheriff tells me you killed one of my top hands. I'd like to know why."

Colter stopped near enough to hear but far enough back so that no one could brace him from behind.

"If you considered Yeager a top hand, you're a sorry judge of character. He was a backshootin', cattle-rustlin' son of a bitch, and if I hadn't shot him, an *honest* court of law would have hanged him sooner or later."

The sheriff bristled at the emphasis Colter had put on the word "honest." "Are you tryin' to say that this town—" The sheriff's words were interrupted as Kittleman placed his hand on his shoulder.

"I'll do the talkin', Bill. I hear this man sayin' that he knew Yeager before and that Yeager rustled some of his cattle. Yeager must have known this fella was after him, and that's why he tried to ambush him. Is that about it?"

"I thought *you* might be able to tell *me*," Colter replied. "He worked for you."

Duke stepped out from behind Kittleman and dropped his hand to a spot where it hovered just above the walnut stock of his gun. "I don't like what you're insinuatin' about Mr. Kittleman, cowboy."

Colter coolly studied Duke's scowling features. Then, with a flickering glance at Kittleman, he looked back again at Duke and spoke. "As I said before, Mr. Kittleman, you must be a sorry judge of character. You ought to keep this one on a leash."

Duke's eyes flashed hatred. "Why you—"

"Duke!" Kittleman bellowed. "I'll handle this."

Duke stepped back slightly behind Kittleman and stared sullenly at Colter.

"I'd like to know what you meant by your insinuation that I must have put Yeager up to his bushwhacking attempt," Kittleman snapped.

"No one knew I was coming to Charleston except the person who wrote the telegram and the guy that sent it. I figure the telegraph agent must have told you or at least one of your boys that I might be comin' here."

"What possible interest could your coming to Charleston have for me—or for any of my boys, for that matter?" Kittleman asked.

"That's what I hope to find out," Colter replied. "The name 'Colter Haines' wouldn't have meant anything to Yeager. It was just a coincidence that we met again. I caught him rustlin' cattle when I worked for Charley Goodnight up in Colorado, but he didn't know who I was other than just somebody he swapped lead with."

"And you figure I sent him outside of town to bushwhack you. Is that it?"

"You said it. I didn't," Colter answered.

"Let me take him, boss," Duke urged, pushing forward.

"You stay out of this, fat gut. Nobody rattled your cage," Colter said.

Duke lunged and made a grab to pin Colter's arms to his side. Colter dodged and drove a powerful left deep into Duke's flabby midsection. In a smooth follow-up, he drew his Colt and hit Duke neatly along side the temple with the barrel. Duke dropped like a poled ox. Colter swung the muzzle of his .45 around to cover the crowd. His actions had been so fast everyone was taken by surprise. Satisfied that no one would try to follow Duke's clumsy lead, he holstered the gun.

"I guess maybe we've had enough talk for one day. You'll probably want to get his head sewed up," Colter said.

"I don't think we have anything further to say to each other," Kittleman answered. "I didn't know a thing about a bushwhacking attempt until the sheriff here sent word that you'd killed Yeager."

"What about Jack's death?" Colter asked.

Kittleman's face clouded. "As far as I know he shot a farmer named Kramer, and Kramer shot him. Pure and simple."

"There's a reason behind everything, Kittleman. Very few things are pure and simple," Colter replied.

John Kittleman bristled. It was the first time he'd been called Kittleman without the respected tag of Mr. in front of it for a long time, and he didn't like it. "We've got a nice town here, Haines, and we don't want somebody bringin' trouble into it. Folks here get along, and I suggest you do the same."

"And if I don't?" Colter asked.

Kittleman just glared without saying a word.

Colter supplied the words. "I get backshot or run out like the others. Yeah, it's a nice town, all right . . . if you don't mind bein' pushed around." He glanced at the sheriff and at Hank Alcott. "Or lickin' a few boots."

Sheriff Thompson made a move toward his gun. "Haines, I'm placin' you under—"

"Hold it, Sheriff!" Colter commanded. His voice had power and an edge to it. His Colt .45 appeared in his hand as if by magic. "Don't be a damned fool. You don't want to die for Kittleman. We both know you can't throw a man in jail just because he speaks out. This country's still free as far as I know."

Kittleman touched the sheriff's arm. "He's right, Bill. I don't like him and you don't like him, but he's right."

"Then get your business finished and get out," the sheriff ordered. "I'll give you til tomorrow night."

"I'll take as long as I need," Colter answered.

"When I'm satisfied, I'll leave, not before." He holstered his gun smoothly, coolly, and backed toward the door.

Thompson's deputy, a lanky nineteen-year-old, stepped out from the crowd. "Haines, I'm takin' you in."

Colter glanced at the sheriff.

"Jimmy, you damned idiot, get over here and shut up," Thompson thundered.

"He can't talk to you like that," Jimmy yelled. "Haines, I'm callin' you."

Colter's voice was steady and low. "Back off, kid. You're over your head."

Jimmy reached for his gun, but Colter's bullet smashed into the cylinder, knocking the weapon from his grasp before it had even cleared leather. Jimmy screamed and grabbed his bleeding hand, pushing the nearly severed finger that hung from a piece of skin back into place.

Colter swung his .45 around, but no one moved. They knew they were outmatched.

"I'm sorry kid," Colter said.

"It was a lucky shot," Jimmy mumbled, fighting back the tears.

"You horse's ass," the sheriff growled. "He could have killed you."

Duke groaned at the sound of the shot and slowly rose to a sitting position, holding his throbbing head.

Kittleman spoke. "Let's get these two to the doctor."

"You draw that gun one more time in this town, Haines, and I'll roast you over a slow fire," the sheriff said.

"That's Apache-style, Sheriff. That's a kind of fighting I know somethin' about. See you." Colter backed out the door and headed for the undertaker's parlor.

Haggerty's Undertaking Parlor was sparsely furnished with the accoutrements of his profession. Several bolts of faded white linen gathered dust alongside a clean one that had just been used. Two models of caskets were on display, one of pine painted black, and the other an unpainted oak. The odor of fresh-cut wood permeated the combination office-parlor when Jacob Haggerty opened the rear door that led to his carpentry shop. The caller's bell above Colter's head still carried a faint ringing sound as the old man brushed the sawdust from his apron. He was a small bandy-legged Irishman who spoke with a brogue that refused to diminish even after twenty years of frontier living.

"Are you in need of a casket, lad?" He ran his hand lovingly along the lid of the unpainted oak. "Imported all the way from the hills of Texas. Solid oak it is, and for a wee bit extra, I'd line it with an aromatic cedar so delicate in fragrance that your friends and acquaintances will be fightin' to be invited to the wake."

Colter smiled. "I'm not shopping. I just wanted to ask you a few questions about my brother, Jack Haines."

Haggerty's face lit up with glee. "So you're the one, are you?" He stuck out his hand. "I'd like to thank you for the business this mornin' . . . even though it was only a pine box. The likes of that one didn't deserve Haggerty's finest. So, you're young Jack Haines' brother, are you? He was a good lad, God rest his soul. Now, what can I do for you?"

"Do you have his . . . effects? His gun or anything from his pockets?"

"The sheriff took those—for evidence, he said. I've got the bullet that killed him, though. 'Twas hangin' by a wee bit of skin just inside the front of his shirt." Haggerty walked to a small desk and took the spent slug from a drawer. "You're welcome to it if you'd like."

"Thanks," Colter said, glancing at the lead slug briefly and then putting it in his shirt pocket. "Was Jack's bill taken care of, or do I owe you some money?"

"His horse was sold by the town council, and they paid me for services rendered," Haggerty replied. "Will you be in town long, lad?"

"I don't know," Colter answered. "It depends."

"Well, I'll order more lumber anyways," Haggerty said, his face creasing into a grin.

"Is there a land office in town?"

"Aye. There's one next to the gunsmith about three streets down."

"Thanks," Colter said. "You've been a big help."

"And so have you, me boy, and so have you," Haggerty answered.

As Colter emerged from Haggerty's Undertaking Parlor, he saw Sheridan Mason waving to him from a block away. The editor was puffing as he arrived.

"I heard about the set-to you had with the sheriff's deputy. That's not exactly what I'd call a start toward building goodwill."

"The sheriff ought to know better than to pick a hotheaded kid for a deputy anyhow," Colter answered.

"I was down at the freight office checking on a paper shipment, and I missed the whole thing," Sheridan said, his voice showing disappointment.

"There wasn't too much happening. I had a few words with Kittleman, cracked Duke on the head with my gun, and shot the deputy sheriff," Colter said wryly.

Sheridan laughed, enjoying Colter's sense of humor. Then, becoming more serious, he said, "I don't think young Jimmy will give you any more trouble, but Duke's another story. You wounded his pride in front of Kittleman's boys. Making a man look foolish in front of his friends is a hell of a lot more serious than putting a lump on his head. He'll stew about that for a bit, and then he'll try to get even.''

"Yeah," Colter added. "Amos said he was a mean one."

"What did you think of Kittleman?"

Colter's eyes narrowed in thought. "There's somethin' strange about that man. He seemed genuinely surprised when I more or less accused him of sending Yeager out to bushwhack me. And he wasn't the least bit edgy when I asked him about Jack's death."

"Jack's death seems pretty cut and dried," Sheridan added. "He *was* having trouble with Kramer before the shooting."

Colter shook his head. "I don't know. Kittleman doesn't quite fit the picture I put together from what Amos told me about him. There are some pieces missing."

Sheridan nodded. "I tend to agree with you. From what I know about the man, I wouldn't call John Kittleman the type of fellow who'd murder or bushwhack somebody. It just isn't his style. Where are you headed now?"

"Thought I'd pick up Jack's gun from the sheriff and then go down to the land office and look around."

"I'll pick up Jack's gun for you. You'd better stay away from the sheriff for a while."

"Thanks," Colter said. "I'll see you later."

"What do you expect to find at the land office?" Sheridan's voice showed interest.

Colter shrugged. "I just want to look at a map or two."

As Colter headed down the street, Sheridan set out for the sheriff's office.

7

Colter stepped into the land office and looked at the large map of the Arizona Territory on the wall behind the counter. The area around Charleston had been enlarged into a map of its own and was tacked up next to the territorial map.

The clerk glanced up from his desk. "Can I help you?"

"I think so," Colter answered. "I'd like to get some information on my brother's ranch."

"What's his name?"

"Jack Haines," Colter replied. "I'm his only surviving kin, so I guess the place legally belongs to me now."

The clerk dug through a file cabinet and pulled a description of the ranch and a small replica of the Charleston map from an envelope. "It seems to me that ranch changed hands about a month ago." He studied the papers and then nodded slowly. "Uh huh! I thought so. Yeah, Mr. Rupert Stull bought that place about . . . well, it's been just about a month ago. I could have sworn Kittleman bought that place." He shrugged. "I guess that's because he's bought so many others."

"Let me see that paper," Colter said. The signature on it was definitely not Jack's handwriting. Whoever this Rupert Stull was, he had to be found and made to answer a hell of a lot of questions. "Thanks a lot,"

Colter replied, handing the paper back to the clerk. "How much does this Kittleman fella own anyways?"

"I don't really know, but it must be at least ten thousand acres. Seems like half the deeds in this town have Mr. Kittleman's name on them. That's what made me think he'd bought your brother's place."

"What was the date on that paper? I forgot to look," Colter said.

"The twenty-first of May."

Cynthia's telegram said Jack had been killed on the twentieth.

"You got an extra map of Charleston that I can have?"

The clerk looked over his glasses at Colter. "It'll cost you twelve cents."

"I think I can scrape together that much," Colter said, taking a quarter from his pocket. As the clerk handed him his map and his change, Colter spoke again. "You wouldn't mind just kind of sketchin' out the boundary of Mr. Kittleman's ranch on this map for me, would you? I reckon that's about the biggest ranch I've ever heard of."

The clerk smiled. "It's a nice-size ranch, but it isn't anything compared to a ranch I heard of in Texas. That one's over a million acres. The western boundary along the New Mexico border is a hundred miles long."

Colter whistled. "It just doesn't seem right for one man to own so much land while others are lucky to have a few acres."

"Well, that ranch is owned by a bunch of investors and not just one man. Give me that map and I'll draw you a rough sketch of the Bar K—that's Kittleman's brand."

He took Colter's map and drew a line along the perimeter of Kittleman's ranch. Then, he shaded in a half-dozen smaller squares. "These are quarter sections, 160 acres. Some of them were just bought by

Mr. Kittleman and they'll become part of the Bar K Ranch.'' He put a small X in the center of one of the shaded squares. "This was your brother's ranch, but as I said, it now belongs to Mr. Stull. That one on the left is owned by Mr. Alcott, the storekeeper. He bought it from Mrs. Kramer right after. . ." The clerk gulped. "Right after he died."

Colter put the map in his pocket. "Much obliged for your help."

"I'm just sorry I had to tell you that you don't have any inheritance coming to you," the clerk responded.

Colter walked out and headed for the telegraph office. It was time to find out who the clerk had talked to after he'd sent Cynthia's telegram.

The clerk was seated with his back to the door when Colter entered. He didn't bother to turn around but spoke over his shoulder. "Be with you in just a minute." He continued sorting papers.

Colter spoke. "Mr. Kittleman wants to know if Miss Dobbs has sent any more telegrams."

"No, she hasn't," the clerk said, "but if she does, I'll let him know just like I did the last"—he spun his swivel chair around on the word—"time." As the sound was dying in his throat, he stared at Colter. "Who are you? You're not one of Mr. Kittleman's hands."

Colter smiled. "You're right! I'm Colter Haines, the one you sent that telegram to. Now, I'd like to know just who it was you talked to after you sent that telegram, because Kittleman didn't know anything about it."

"Who I talked to is nobody's business but mine," the clerk snapped. "Now get out of here. I'm busy." He spun his chair around with his back to Colter and continued sorting papers.

Colter spun the chair back around with his left hand

and drew his gun with his right. The chair stopped with the clerk staring down the muzzle of Colter's .45.

"Now, pay attention 'cause I'm only going to say this once. Who did you talk to? Was it Duke . . . Yeager . . . Thompson?"

The clerk's eyes lit up at the mention of the sheriff's name. "It was Thompson. That's who it was."

Colter thumbed the hammer back. "You're a liar. You got one more chance. Now, I want the truth, or I'll give you a third eye right between the other two."

The clerk paled and trembled noticeably. Swallowing dryly, he tried to look away, but Colter touched the barrel to his cheek and nudged it gently.

"Don't make me do this again. It's got a hair trigger."

"I told Duke. He said Mr. Kittleman wanted to know."

Colter eased the hammer back down and holstered his gun. Giving the clerk's cheek a light pat, he smiled. "You're a good boy. Stay that way, and don't tell anyone you talked to me."

He turned and left the office deep in thought. What did Duke do with the information the clerk had given him about the telegram? He certainly hadn't given it to his boss because Kittleman was genuinely surprised when Colter had confronted him about Yeager's bushwhacking attempt. Duke had used the information for his own advantage, but what was his purpose? It had to be a gain of some sort. The obvious prize was Jack's ranch, but he had seen his brother's place, and it was certainly nothing to kill two people over, not to mention an attempt to kill a third one . . . himself. There had to be something else. Maybe Jack was mixed up in some kind of crooked deal and he was shot because he knew too much. That made a lot more sense to Colter. Well, whatever it was, he'd find it out.

He stopped in front of Levi Ormand's gunsmith shop

and thought about the slug that Haggerty, the undertaker, had given him. He stepped inside, and Levi, a wiry, energetic little man, smiled and got up from his workbench. "What can I do for you?"

Colter dropped the slug on the counter. "What kind of gun you reckon this came from?"

Levi picked it up and stepped to his bench for a magnifying glass. Studying the slug carefully, he walked back to the counter. "Looks like a fifty-two-caliber Spencer. They went out of production back in '69. Company went bankrupt. Don't see many of those around nowadays. Everybody uses a Winchester."

"Do you know anybody around here that has one?"

"Not offhand. Why?"

"Just curious."

"Last box of shells I sold for a gun like that was about a year ago."

"Don't happen to remember who bought 'em, do you?"

Levi scratched his head. "By doggies, I can't put my finger on it right now, but it'll come to me. I never forget a face, but I ain't too good on names. You gonna be around town for a while, Mr., ah. . ."

"Haines. Colter Haines. Yes, I'll be staying at the Imperial Hotel, room ten. If you happen to remember who it was, I'd be much obliged if you'd stop by and tell me."

"I certainly will if I can get a handle on it," Levi said with a smile.

Colter walked back toward the sheriff's office.

Sheridan Mason hailed him from across the street. "Here's your brother's gun. I was just heading down to the Imperial to leave it with the clerk if you weren't in."

Colter took Jack's gun and looked it over carefully.

Sheridan watched him with growing interest. "Well, did you find out anything that was useful?"

Colter grinned. "Yeah, I uncovered a few bits and pieces. Know anybody that has an old Spencer rifle, a fifty-two-caliber?"

Sheridan's eyes narrowed. "Why? Does that have special meaning to you?"

"It could."

Sheridan rubbed his chin thoughtfully. "I've seen one of them on someone's saddle, but I'll be danged if I can remember where or whose horse it was hanging on. That was a fine weapon, very accurate. I carried one back in the war. You still think Jack was murdered? You aim to pursue that idea? It'll only cause trouble, you know."

"Yeah, I not only think he was murdered, I know it. And yes, I am going to pursue it."

"You can't always depend on information Amos Carson gives, you know. He doesn't like Kittleman, and he'll do everything he can to implicate him."

"I'm not depending on just Amos' word." Colter took the lead bullet from his shirt pocket. "Haggerty gave me this. It's a fifty-two-caliber Spencer slug. It came out of the front of Jack's chest. It was hangin' on by a little piece of skin. That means it had to have come through his back. Now if Jack killed this fella Kramer like they say, Kramer wouldn't have been able to shoot Jack in the back. And if Kramer shot Jack first, Jack wouldn't have been able to turn around, draw his gun, and shoot Kramer—not with a hole in him a slug like this makes. Besides, if Jack had been shot at close range like the sheriff said, the bullet would have gone clean through. Jack was shot from a distance, not handgun range."

Sheridan's face lost its dour expression, and his eyes burned with excitement. He smelled a good story in the making. "Well, I'd say you certainly have uncovered a few bits and pieces. What you say makes sense, damned good sense. What I'm wondering now is, was

Sheriff Thompson telling the truth about where he found Jack and Kramer, and did someone kill both of the men and set it up so that Thompson was taken in by it all? Or . . . is Bill Thompson mixed up in this murder and is trying to protect himself? It's going to be pretty interesting finding out the answers to these questions.''

Colter nodded grimly. ''I aim to ask him a few questions right now, and he'd better have some answers.''

Sheridan raised an eyebrow. ''It could be pretty dangerous for you.''

''I'm not worried.''

''I am,'' Sheridan said, grinning. ''Wait a minute and I'll go with you.'' He stepped inside his newspaper office and took a gun from his desk, a .41-caliber Colt Thunderer, and tucked it inside his belt. Then, walking outside, he smiled. ''Now, I feel better. Let's go.''

Sheriff Thompson sat behind his desk with his feet propped up and his eyes closed, puffing on a cigar. He was irritated by the sudden appearance of Colter Haines, and he didn't like the idea of having Jack's death gone over with a currycomb. There were things about the death of both Jack and Kramer that had bothered him, but he had accepted Mrs. Kramer's story that both men had quarreled earlier in the day as a logical lead up to a double killing. However, there was the nagging problem of that unfired shell in the breech of Kramer's rifle. If Haines had shot Kramer in the head first, Kramer wouldn't have been able to fire and chamber another round. Of course, if Kramer had shot Haines first, he could have chambered another round in case he needed it. That had to be the explanation. It made sense.

He glanced between the toes of his boots and saw Colter and Sheridan Mason at the door. He dropped his feet to the floor just as they entered. Taking the cigar from his mouth, he glared at Colter. "What in the hell do *you* want?"

A faint trace of a smile crossed Colter's face. Turning to Sheridan, he said. "Now, that's not the kind of greeting one should expect from a public servant, is it, Sheridan?"

"I ain't nobody's servant, Haines. What do you want with me?" he growled.

"I was just wondering if you have Mr. Kramer's rifle here. I'd like to see it if you have."

The sheriff eyed Colter suspiciously. "Yeah, I've got it, but what in the hell business is it of yours if I do?"

Sheridan spoke. "Bill, when a murder has been committed, the man has a right to ask questions to clear things up in his own mind."

"There wasn't no murder. It was plain that they shot and killed each other."

"The gun," Colter said. "I'd like to see it."

Thompson rose and walked back to the gun rack that stood against the wall. He pulled a lever action Winchester .30-30 rifle from its peg and walked back to the two men. "Is this your idea, Mason, so you can write some tomfool story and sell more papers?"

"No," Colter said, taking the rifle, "I thought of it all by myself. Now I want to show you something, Sheriff. You see this slug?" He held up the bullet Haggerty had given him. "Does this look like it came from this rifle?"

Thompson glared at the slug and took it from Colter's hand. He turned it around several times. "Hell, no, it didn't. This here's at least a fifty caliber."

"Fifty-two-caliber to be exact," Colter said. "This slug was taken out of my brother's chest. It was held in place by a thin piece of skin. That means Jack was shot in the back from quite a distance away. How close were Jack and Kramer together when you found them?''

The sheriff's eyes clouded as the realization began to dawn that the nagging loose ends of that double shooting was something he should have taken care of a long time ago. He should have asked himself the same questions Colter was pressing on him now. ''They were just across the fence from each other . . . maybe eight or ten feet apart,'' he said.

''Would you say that at a distance of ten feet a fifty-two-caliber bullet would go clear through a man or just push through to the skin on the other side?''

''I see what you're getting at. Somebody killed Jack somewheres else and brought him back to where I found him. Is that what you're thinkin'?''

''Yeah, it makes sense to me.''

''Well, it sure as hell don't to me. Who would be fool enough to shoot a man and then carry him a mile or two and dump him someplace else? And why would he kill Kramer too? He could have left your brother out in a canyon somewheres, and he wouldn't have been found for a month or two. And why'd he want to blame it on Kramer for? It just don't make any sense at all.''

''It does if you want a man's property. Both men had a spread that somebody wanted bad enough to kill them for.''

''I don't buy that! Neither one of them places were worth a hoot. Kramer could barely support his family on the place, and your brother hadn't done a thing to his spread but build a shack on it.''

''Well, it has to be something like that . . . some reason for killing them both.''

''Well, I'll admit there are a few things that just don't twang the string in the right way, but I sure can't go along with that wild scheme of yours. I can't think of a single suspect that would benefit from the deaths of Kramer and your brother."

"I've got some pretty good hunches," Colter said.

"Now, don't you go shootin' somebody just 'cause you got suspicions. It'll have to be proved in a court of law that whoever it is is guilty, and if that's the case, I'll lock him up my own self."

"What if it turns out to be Kittleman?" Sheridan asked.

"We'll cross that creek when we come to it," Thompson added.

8

Colter was crossing the street to the Imperial Hotel when a soft melodious voice called out his name. He turned and saw Cynthia coming out of the store.

"I'm glad you're still walking around. Most men that have had a run-in with John Kittleman in the past haven't fared too well," she said.

Colter smiled. "So far it's been all bark."

"Those who have come out on the short end of the stick with Mr. Kittleman can testify to his bite. Don't take him for granted. He's a hard and angry man."

"I'm not exactly a tenderfoot, you know."

She smiled and her whole face lit up. He was surprised at how good it made him feel to have such a beautiful woman smile at him.

"Really?" she said, a tease in her voice. "Why, I could have sworn I saw some damp spots behind your ears when you left here earlier. You certainly fooled me, Mr. Haines."

"If you keep calling me Mr. Haines instead of Colter, I'll have to show you how angry I can really get."

"Oh," she said, "I'm terribly sorry about that. Is there anything I can do to make amends?" Her voice was still mocking.

He looked her directly in the eyes with such intense concentration she suddenly found herself floundering as to how she should react.

"Yes," he said slowly, drawing out the word.

She blushed a deep shade of red.

He smiled and added quickly. "I'd like you to have dinner with me."

"Well, I . . . hadn't really planned. . ."

"Good!" he interrupted. "If you haven't planned dinner, then there'll be no food to go to waste. I really do hate to eat alone, don't you?"

"Well, yes, I do, but. . ."

"Then it's settled. You tell me where you'd like to go. I'm not very familiar with this town yet." He took her arm and started walking down the street.

"Are you always so direct?"

He smiled. "I am where it really counts."

"And this evening's meal really counts. Is that it?" Her fluster had disappeared and her breathing was returned to normal.

His face became serious. "Yes," he replied solemnly. "I'm conducting an investigation, and you're one of my star witnesses. I'll need to ask you some very important questions . . . over dinner, of course."

"Of course," she answered, and they both laughed. "Good heavens!" she exclaimed suddenly. "We're going in the wrong direction. The restaurant is back that way."

"I know," Colter said, looking at her again with great intensity. "I figured if we went this way, we'd have a longer stroll, and I kinda like that idea."

She glanced down at the boardwalk, but he could see the edges of her cheeks tinged with red again, and he smiled.

All during the meal he was content just to watch her every move and save his talking until she had finished eating. She knew she was being watched carefully . . . no, studied intently would fit the description better, and she loved it. It was irritating to her that she couldn't control her blushing, but his presence did strange things to her, stirred feelings that were not so much dormant as just unused. No one had ever made her feel as she felt now. Even Jack, as nice as he was at first, had failed to stir up the inner excitement this rugged, handsome man across the table from her was managing to do by just sitting and smiling.

"What was it you wanted to talk about that was so important?" she asked, hoping that the question would get him to thinking of other things besides her.

"I can't remember when I've enjoyed myself more," he said, signalling the waiter for some coffee.

"Yes, it was a good meal," she commented.

"I meant the company, but the food was good too."

Darn him, she thought, he's done it again. She could feel a slight flush of color rise to her cheeks. "Thank you," she said. "That's a nice compliment. Now, Mr. Hai, ah, Colter, what are those important questions?"

Colter waited until the waiter refilled their cups and left before he spoke. "I think I know where the box and the letter Jack left for me have disappeared to!"

"Where?" Her eyes sparkled with excitement.

"Hank Alcott took them."

A frown crossed her face. "I don't believe that. Mr. Alcott is a very nice man. What on earth would he want to do something like that for? He doesn't know you, and what's more, he wouldn't take anything that didn't belong to him."

"Hank Alcott is the man who bought the Kramer place after Kramer was killed, and somebody named Stull took over Jack's ranch."

"So? That doesn't make him a thief, does it?"

"I think it might. This is how I've got it figured. Jack was onto something important, probably mixed up in it, if I know Jack. Whatever it was, he was murdered because he knew too much."

"Jack was shot by Mr. Kramer, and that's not exactly murder. After all, they killed each other. Mrs.

Kramer said they'd argued a couple of hours before the shootings.''

"They didn't kill each other. Jack was shot in the back with a fifty-two-caliber Spencer rifle from quite a ways off. Kramer's gun is a thirty-caliber Winchester.''

"How do you know this?" she asked.

"The undertaker gave me the bullet he took out of Jack's chest, and the gunsmith told me the caliber of the slug.''

"How does Mr. Alcott figure in this?"

"I think he's mixed up in whatever's going on. After Jack was killed, they knew they'd have to do something to keep the next of kin from getting his ranch and to keep whatever it was they were involved in a secret. That's why I think Alcott took the box and the letter. Kittleman's foreman, Duke, is mixed up in it too. He's the one the telegraph clerk told about the telegram you sent to me.''

"Then who is this Mr. Stull who bought Jack's ranch?"

"I don't know yet, but I know he didn't buy the ranch. I saw the signature on the deed, and it wasn't Jack's.''

"Is Mr. Kittleman involved in this mess?"

"I don't believe so. He seems like an honest man to me. Oh, I know he doesn't like homesteaders or sheepherders—few cattlemen do—but I don't think he'd kill people in cold blood to have his way. He'd push them, or burn them out, or rough them up, but I think he'd draw the line on outright killing.''

"Have you told the sheriff about this?"

"I've told him only about the way Jack was killed. He knows I'm right.''

"What's he going to do about it?"

"I guess he's going to see what he can find out. He seemed sincere enough.''

"He's Kittleman's man."

"I know it, but Sheridan Mason is on my side, and the press is a powerful weapon when it's turned against somebody. Sheriff Thompson's well aware of that also."

Cynthia rose from the table. "I'd better be getting back. Mr. Alcott wanted me to help him take inventory tonight."

After Colter had walked Cynthia back to Alcott's store, he headed for Bascomb's Saloon.

The bartender smiled broadly as Colter entered. "Evenin' Colter." Colter nodded. "How about a beer on me?"

"Sounds like a good idea," Colter said.

Bascomb drew a beer and scraped off the head with the side of his hand. Then, carrying the glass back to Colter, he set it down on the bar and started the conversation. "I seen young Jimmy Wilson a while ago. Looked kinda peaked with his hand all wrapped up and his arm in a sling."

"Jimmy Wilson?"

"That young fool deputy you shot."

Colter shook his head. "Thompson ought to know better than to hire a green kid to do sheriff's work. He'll get himself killed unless he smartens up in a hurry."

"Well," Bascomb said, chuckling, "he's gonna have plenty of time for thinkin' about how he was gonna make a name for himself drawin' his iron against the likes of you."

A man entered the batwing doors brushing dust from his clothes. He was dressed in a broadcloth suit that had a definite tailored look to it. He smiled when he saw Bascomb and Colter looking at him. "Good evening. You wouldn't happen to have a cold beer in this establishment, would you?"

Bascomb raised an eyebrow. "Ain't nothin' cold in

this town that I know of, 'cept the banker's heart. I got a beer that ain't exactly frosty, but it'll cut the dust from your throat.''

"Sounds good. Would you join me, sir, and you also, bartender? I hate to drink by myself.''

Colter nodded. "Thank you.''

Bascomb drew three beers and carried them down the bar, then joined Colter as the newcomer raised his glass in a toast. "May the good Lord see to it that the stagecoach gets new springs. My kidneys are about gone.'' He downed half of the glass before stopping. Then, sticking out his hand, he said, "I'm Alfred Peters. I'm a mining engineer from Phoenix.''

"What in the world you doin' in Charleston?'' Bascomb asked.

"I'm on my way down to Mexico to inspect some silver mines for a client of mine that wants to do some investing. I'm certainly glad to be able to make an overnight stop here. That four-wheel torture rack I've been riding in is an abomination.''

Colter reached into his shirt pocket for the lead slug Haggerty had given him. When he pulled it out, the blue rock Johnny had given him fell to the floor and bounced to halt near Alfred Peter's foot. Colter ignored it for the moment and showed the slug to Bascomb. "You wouldn't happen to know a fella that carries a fifty-two-caliber Spencer in his saddle boot, would you?''

Bascomb looked at the slug. "I don't get much of a chance to go outside once I open them doors. A fella could be ridin' a camel and I'd never know it, let alone what kind of rifle he might be a-carryin'. But . . . I can ask around, kind of sly like, and see what I can find out for you, if you want me to.''

"I'd be beholden to you if you would,'' Colter answered. He started for the door when Alfred Peters called to him.

"A moment sir." Colter stopped. Peters came up and handed him the blue rock he had dropped. "I believe this is yours. It fell from your pocket. Is there much of this stuff around here?"

"You mean blue rock?" Colter asked as he started walking again.

Peters nodded. "Yes." He followed Colter outside.

"I don't know. I think there's some on my brother's ranch." He dug in his pocket and brought out the green and blue rocks he had found in Jack's cabin. "Well, this one's green, but the blue one's the same as that one, isn't it? I got these out at his place."

Peters examined the rocks. "The green one is malachite and the blue is azurite, sometimes called blue malachite. These samples have a great deal of copper in them. If there's much of this on his ranch, your brother might become a wealthy man. I'd be glad to run some tests when I return from Mexico if you'd like. I didn't want to say anything about these rocks inside because bartenders are generally great talkers, and it's best to keep something like this quiet until you've got it all locked up."

"I'm much obliged for both your offer and your discretion. My name's Colter Haines. I'd like to have you stop here on your way back to Phoenix. By that time I'll know exactly what my brother has, and maybe we can do business together."

"I'll look forward to it," Peters said, shaking Colter's extended hand.

"Good night," Colter said as Peters went back inside to finish his beer. He stood for a few moments digesting what the engineer had told him. The man had supplied the key to the problem that had been plaguing Colter since he'd first come to town. It had to be the scheme that Jack was mixed up in, the missing ingredient that gave sense and reason to what had happened. Jack was killed because there was a big copper deposit somewhere, and he must have known the location of it. It might be on Jack's ranch, or Kramer's, or even on Kittleman's place. In fact, it could be on all three of them. That would make the stakes high enough to turn somebody into a killer so the profits wouldn't have to be split so many ways. Kramer was probably killed to supply a reason for Jack's death. The thing to do was to ride out to Jack's ranch in the morning and see what he could find out. He'd look the place over from one end of the spread to the other. Now that he knew what to look for, it shouldn't be too hard to find.

Colter turned and headed down the dark boardwalk toward the Imperial Hotel. As he crossed the street, a shot rang out from an alley and he felt the bullet whine by just inches from his face. He sprinted to the cover of a darkened building and stood with his back to the wall and his gun drawn. Moving along the wall, he came to the alley where the shot had come from. He peered around the corner cautiously and another shot split the air, the slug embedding itself in the wood near his head. He leaped into the alley and fired in the direction of the tip of fire he'd seen when the shell had exploded. There was a noise of someone falling over some boxes and then footsteps pounding down the alley. He fired once more in the general direction of the sound. There was a moment of silence and then the clatter of horses' hooves against the hard-packed dirt of the street. After they'd faded into the night, Colter rose and stepped back into the street. The sound of running feet spun him around toward Bascomb's Saloon. It was Sheriff Thompson.

"What's goin' on, Haines?"

"Somebody tried to bushwhack me from this alley. I fired at him, but he got away. He made a lot of noise back there. I don't know whether I hit him or not. It sounded like he fell over some boxes or something, then jumped on his horse and hightailed it out.''

"Don't have any ideas about who it was, do you?''

"No, but I'll find out.''

"Just don't do anything that's illegal, or I'll have to run you in.''

"Yeah, I know.''

"I ain't never seen a man stir up as much trouble as you have, and it ain't even been twelve hours since you got to town.''

"Just a born hell-raiser, Sheriff,'' Colter said, grinning. "Good night now.''

Sheriff Thompson watched as Colter disappeared in the darkness. He'd have to ride out and see Kittleman in the morning and tell him about the new development in the Haines-Kramer case. He'd also tell Kittleman about the attempt on Colter's life and suggest that Kittleman keep a tight rein on his cowhands for a while. Kittleman wouldn't like to be told what to do, but, the sheriff reasoned, a man must look out for himself. He didn't mind looking the other way when Kittleman's hands roughed up a few nesters, but Jack Haines was no homesteader, and he had been murdered, backshot, and that made it a whole new story. If he didn't start showing a little backbone now, it could become a lot more difficult to do later on. Also, there was the power of Sheridan Mason's newspaper, and he certainly didn't want that turned against him. If he had to choose between Kittleman and Mason as an ally, the printed word was a hell of a lot stronger than a rancher's promise. He knew John Kittleman would throw him away like a worn-out horseshoe as soon as his usefulness was at an end.

Colter crossed the street and stepped up on the boardwalk in front of the Imperial Hotel.

"Hey!'' someone called softly from the darkness at the side of the hotel.

Colter drew his gun and walked toward the sound.

"No need for gun," the voice said. It was thick with Indian phrasing and accent.

"Step to the corner so I can see who I'm talking to," Colter said. "Who are you, and what do you want?"

The man moved until a slender shaft of soft lamplight slicing through the darkness from the hotel lobby played across his ancient face. "My name Chirtua. Man who shoot in alley ride Bar K horse."

"Did you see the man? Do you know who it was?"

"Not see man. See horse. Him ride grulla with Bar K on hip."

"How is it that you saw the horse but not the man?" Colter asked suspiciously.

"Him have horse tied behind store. I feel saddlebags for maybe . . . drink. I see brand on horse. No see man. I go to street. Hear gun boom-boom. Man run around corner, jump on horse, ride that way." He pointed to the north in the direction of Kittleman's Bar K Ranch.

Chirtua. The name began to nag at Colter's memory until he remembered Cynthia's words. Jack used to hang around an old Indian when he occasionally went on a drinking binge. "You knew my brother, Jack Haines. You and him used to have a drink together once in a while, didn't you?"

Chirtua's leathery face softened as he grinned, exposing many rotted teeth. "Jack . . . good white man. Treat Chirtua good . . . like brother." He squinted as he studied Colter's face. "You no look like Jack."

"You no look like Sitting Bull," Colter said.

Chirtua's brows knitted in bewilderment for a moment, then he chuckled, a low rumbling sound that started deep inside and came out in a staccato "huh-huh-huh," almost mechanical in tone.

"Did you ever go out to my brother's ranch?"

"Yes. I go two . . . three times maybe. Bar K man . . . Duke . . . him say don't come no more Jack's ranch. I no go."

"When did Duke tell you this? How long ago?"

"Maybe one moon."

"Was this after Jack had been shot?"

"Maybe same time."

"You mean the same day? Were you out at Jack's ranch that day?"

"Me see smoke come from Jack's ranch. I go see. Duke, him ride up and beat me with quirt. Him say, 'You go! Stay away from ranch—no come back!' I go . . . See?" He leaned forward and showed Colter a scar running diagonally across his cheek from earlobe to mouth.

"Yeah, I see a lot of things. Here." He pulled a dollar from his pocket and gave it to the old man. "Buy yourself a bottle."

"You good white man . . . like brother." Chirtua took the money and faded into the darkness.

Colter lay in bed listening to the night sounds that drifted through his half-opened window. Somewhere to the south he heard a coyote cub yapping. The sound brought on a barrage of barking from half a dozen town dogs yearning to be out of their yards running through the scrub. Chirtua's story had added another piece to the potpourri of information he'd gathered about Jack's death. At least now he felt that he knew who had burned Jack's house. Why it was burned was another page to the story he hoped he'd be able to add later. Tomorrow, perhaps, he would find some answers to several questions that plagued him. Tomorrow . . . He drifted into sleep.

9

Colter had just finished breakfast and was having his third cup of coffee when Cynthia came into the restaurant. She spotted him and walked over smiling. He rose and offered her a seat. "This is certainly a pleasant surprise," he said. "Have you had breakfast?"

"Yes, but I'll have coffee with you if you don't mind."

"Mind? I'd feel real put out if you didn't." He signaled for a waiter, who brought another cup and some coffee.

Her smile disappeared. "I heard that someone tried to kill you last night. Do you have any idea who it was?"

Colter nodded. "I've got ideas but no proof. Where was Alcott last night? Was he in the store all the time?"

Cynthia's brows knitted in consternation. "You still believe that he is mixed up some way in Jack's death, don't you?"

"Maybe."

"Well, he was in the store all evening."

"Can you account for every minute of his time? By that I mean, was he in your sight every minute?"

"I was helping him with the inventory. Of *course*, he was there all evening . . . Well, he was out for about ten minutes."

"Where'd he go?"

"Not far. He stepped out in back to talk to an acquaintance of his. I could hear their voices."

"What time was that . . . approximately?"

She shrugged. "I imagine it was about nine-fifteen. The stage from Phoenix had come in about fifteen minutes before that, and it usually arrives at nine o'clock."

"I talked to a man who'd gotten off that stage. I left Bascomb's place about half an hour after that . . . about nine-thirty I guess. That's when someone took a couple of shots at me. Did you see who Alcott talked to or see his horse?"

"No, but I'm sure I'd recognize his voice again if I heard it. He had a very distinct accent. I don't know what kind, but it was very distinct."

"Well, that won't do us any good unless we set you up on the boardwalk and have every cowboy in the territory walk by and tell you a story."

She smiled and was glad, for some unknown reason, that he'd said *us* and *we* in his humorous little suggestion. "That's an interesting idea," she said with exaggerated enthusiasm. "There are lots of men in this area that must have some very exciting stories to tell, and I know they'd be more than willing to share those adventures with a female listener."

"You're too eager," Colter said. "Forget it."

Cynthia finished her coffee with a twinkle in her eyes and reluctantly rose. "I must be going, or I'll be late for work."

Colter left some money on the table and took his hat from the rack. "I'll walk you to the store."

"What have you got planned for the day?" she asked.

"I'm going to ride out to Jack's ranch and then visit the Kramer place. I might even call on Kittleman."

Her face took on a worried expression. "Neither Kittleman nor any of his hands likes you. Do you really think that's a good idea?"

"I've got a special reason for going. I know the kind of horse I'm looking for, and there's a couple of other things I'd like to find out about."

"Please be careful. You've made more than a few enemies since you hit town, and at least one of them has taken a shot at you."

"Yeah, I noticed that," he said, grinning.

She shook her head in exasperation, but she couldn't hold back a smile. She liked his sense of humor. A man that could find humor in a potentially dangerous situation was rare. "Will you have dinner with me this evening? My landlady, Mrs. O'Reilly, is fixing her specialty of corned beef and cabbage, and I thought you might enjoy a home-cooked meal for a change."

"That would pleasure me greatly. Tell Mrs. O'Reilly I hope she's fixin' a big pot, 'cause that's one of my favorites."

"Until tonight, then," she said, and then entered the store.

"I wondered if you was still kickin' around."

Colter turned and a smile spread across his face as Amos Carson pulled up in a wagon with Johnny sitting beside him. "Good to see you again, Amos. Hello, Johnny. How you doin'?"

Johnny grinned. "That's him, Pa."

Amos nodded. "Yeah, that's the man. He asked you how you are."

"Yeah," Johnny said. "How you are." He didn't say it as a question but as a repeat of Amos' words.

Amos smiled at Colter. "From the looks of that little filly I just seen you a-talkin' to, I'd say yore doin' right smart."

Colter beamed. "Yeah, she's quite a beauty, isn't she? Works here in the store. Where can we talk? I've got a few things to tell you."

"Let's go to the blacksmith's. The rim's about ready

to come off that wheel back yonder, and I'd like to git it fixed. Hop on.''

After they'd arrived at the smithy's and Amos had described the work he wanted done, they climbed to the top rail of the blacksmith's corral and sat. Johnny stood, mouth open, gazing at the hot coals in the forge. Colter told Amos everything he had learned since coming to town and everything that had happened to him in that length of time . . . everything but the information about a possible rich copper deposit.

Amos chuckled and shook his head. ''I don't reckon I've ever knowed anybody that could stir up hornet's like you done in such a short time. By doggies I thank you'd charge the fires of hell with a hatful of water, wouldn't you?''

Colter smiled. ''I don't know about that, but when a man's brother has been murdered and his ranch stolen, somebody's got to do somethin' about it.''

''What you aimin' to do now?''

''I'm ridin' out to Jack's ranch to look around. Then I'll go to Kramer's place. I might even ride on Kittleman's land while I'm at it.''

''A man that moves around snakes is apt to git bit. I'd be danged careful about goin' out to Kittleman's spread by myself if I was you . . . lessen you got some snakebite medicine with you. Reckon you'll be comin' back out to the house to stay? Johnny kinda misses you, and . . . well, I wouldn't mind havin' somebody I could talk to neither.''

''I'll have to stick around town for a while. There are just too many loose ends that need tyin' down. I'll come out when I'm done.''

''At least you won't have no bushwhacker tryin' to pick you off in the dark if you're out there with us.''

''I wouldn't be too sure,'' Colter said. ''I just don't want you and Johnny bothered with my troubles. Whoever's behind this has already killed two men, and I don't think he'd hesitate to shoot up your place if he thought I was stayin' there.''

"I ain't afraid of Kittleman or any of his two-bit crew, and that goes double for the peckerhead Duke and that shifty-eyed McQueen that's always ridin' with him.''

"I'll keep that in mind if I start a war," Colter said.

"Has Sheridan Mason done anything to help you at all?''

"Yeah, he went with me to talk to Sheriff Thompson. He's tryin' to be useful.''

"He's about as useful as tits on a boar. What he ought to do is write an article in his paper about Kittleman's land-grabbin' methods. Git some public opinion stirred up. Hell, I could stick a quill up my butt and do back flips and write more articles than that bozo. Calls hisself a newspaper man. Why, for chrissake, he couldn't recognize a good story if Lady Godivy rode down the street with one glued to her ass.''

Colter laughed. "I think you're a bit hard on the old boy. He'll come through okay.''

"Yeah," Amos said with resignation, "and so does a lamb that's a breech birth, but you usually kill the ewe gittin' the little bugger out.''

Colter reined the gelding to a halt and took the map from his pocket. He marked a small X on the spot where Jack's cabin had stood. Then, after he compared map to terrain, he put it back in his pocket and took out the makings of a cigarette. While he rolled himself a smoke, he studied the ground. He decided to ride the perimeter of the ranch, then cut diagonally across the center, then up the west side and diagonally across the center again. That would give him a box pattern with an X drawn across the middle and connecting all four corners. That way he'd cover all the ground. He finished the cigarette and started his ride.

The terrain was hilly but not steep. A small arroyo cut across the northeast corner and carried a slender thread of year-around water along its sandy bottom. Jack was fortunate in that he had water on his land, Colter thought. The land was not suitable for farming. It could be if there was adequate water for irrigation, but there wasn't so most people who homesteaded tried to raise cattle and only grew enough produce to suit their own needs. Along the upper boundary and in the northwest corner where Jack's and Kramer's spreads touched Kittleman's Bar K Ranch, lay an outcrop of rock that rose fifty feet in the air.

After Colter had ridden the entire quarter section without finding anything, he turned back to the outcrop of rock again. Leaving his roan tied at the base of the rock, he climbed up the face to the top and stood looking in all directions. There was an undercut caused by a flash flood on the northern base of the high point Colter was standing on. He went down to investigate.

There was a vein of malachite that cut through the center of the undercut and angled off into the scrub beyond. Colter followed it. The vein thinned out for a ways, then broadened as it angled across Jack's ranch. It didn't lie on the surface except in a few spots, but he was able to follow it fairly well. It cut through the corner of Kramer's ranch and headed into the Kittleman spread. Colter went back and got his horse, then continued to trace the small peaks of the vein as they poked through the sandy topsoil under creosote bushes, through patches of snakeweed, and down a rock-strewn draw. The vein then either petered out or disappeared under a heavier layer of soil, for he could no longer find it. Looking back at the outcrop he had started from, he estimated the vein to be at least a half-mile in length, and there was no telling how wide it was.

If Alfred Peters was right about this green rock having a rich deposit of copper in it, Jack would have stood to earn a fortune if he had lived. Colter rode back and climbed to the top of the big rock. The vein, as near as he could figure, was shaped like the letter J. It started on Jack's ranch and angled in a gentle curve through the corner of Kramer's place, then moved in a fairly straight line across Kittleman's Bar K, disappearing at the top of the letter.

A shot shattered the stillness and the slug hit the rock Colter was leaning against, then ricocheted with a whine into the air on his left. He dropped into a large split in the rock that lay close to his feet and angled back toward his horse. That shot had come from a large-caliber rifle, and he wanted to see whose face the stock was touching. A second shot glanced off a rock near his shoulder and plowed into a sandbank behind him.

Fortunately his horse was tethered behind some rocks that offered protection from the lone gunman. He took his Winchester from the saddle scabbard and moved up the back of the outcrop to get to a higher elevation. Cautiously peering around a boulder, he caught the glint of sunlight reflecting off metal. He took aim and fired. A few seconds later he could hear a horse leaving from the brush behind the area he had shot into.

Moving back down to his horse, Colter stopped in the area where the second shot had slammed into a sandbank, and dug around for a few minutes. He found the slug he was searching for. It came from a .52-caliber Spencer. After putting the slug in his pocket next to its twin, he mounted up and rode to the area where the bushwhacker had been hiding. There was nothing there that he could use. The tracks led in the direction of the Bar K Ranch, and there was no shell casing to be picked up.

He got down and studied the tracks. It had been only

one horse, but that one wouldn't be hard to track. The left front hoof had a tendency to pigeon-toe slightly, and judging from the depth of the tracks, the rider was a large man, or at least a heavy one.

10

Colter stood, with his hair still slightly wet, wearing a clean shirt and smelling of lavender toilet water, in front of Mrs. O'Reilly's door. He could hear the light click of heels on a wood floor and the faint rustle of material swishing around as Cynthia answered the knock. Her face looked clean and well-scrubbed. She wore a blue gingham dress, a blue ribbon, tying her blond hair back away from her face, and she smelled heavenly.

"Come in." She gave him a dazzling smile and stepped aside as he entered. She presented herself in a way that Colter would remember for years to come.

His grin was irrepressible. "I've heard men say that the northern lights are the most beautiful thing they had ever seen. I've heard others say the same thing about a newborn colt, but I'd match you against anything, anytime, anywhere."

Cynthia stepped back into the shadows for a moment to hide the color change, then said, "Thank you. You do have a way with words, Colter. Come in. Mrs. O'Reilly has dinner ready, and I'm sure she'll be putting it on the table in another minute."

Mrs. O'Reilly came into the dining room carrying a large crock serving pot from the kitchen. It was filled with steaming cabbage and corned beef. The table was set for three, and in the center was a large loaf of warm bread just out of the oven.

She was a rotund, apple-cheeked woman whose gray hair was done up in a bun at the back of her head. Her pleasant, friendly face wore a large smile. She set the pot of corned beef and cabbage on the table and extended a short, firm hand to Colter. Her Irish brogue was as thick as Haggerty's. "Welcome to my home, Mr. Haines. Cynthia has spoke of you so many times I feel I know you." She shook hands. "Sit down, sit down. Mind you, it ain't nothin' special, but my late husband, God rest his soul, loved it above all else. I used to fix it for himself at least once a week, and on occasion two or three times by special request."

"It smells absolutely delicious in here," he said.

"She's a wonderful cook," Cynthia added. "And she's fixed a special dessert just for you . . . spiced apple cobbler with whipped cream on it."

Colter sat, and Mrs. O'Reilly immediately filled his plate to capacity before she took her seat. The meal brought back all the early memories of childhood that Colter had been out of touch with for years. Usually he thought about his adopted parents, the Haines, but almost invariably corned beef and cabbage dredged up faded pictures of his real mother and father, and it always made him feel warm inside. He hadn't eaten such a delicious dinner in . . . he'd forgotten just how long it had been. When he'd finished the main course, Mrs. O'Reilly served him a huge bowl of hot, spiced apple cobbler with a big dollop of whipped cream gradually melting on the crust. He finished it off in record time.

"Why don't you folks go out and set in the swing on the side porch and I'll bring you some Irish coffee?"

"Mrs. O'Reilly, if I weren't already promised, I'd ask you to marry me," Colter said, grinning. "A woman who cooks as good as you do should have a good man at the table to appreciate it."

"That's what I keep tellin' her highness, here," she answered, nodding at Cynthia. "I thank you for the compliment. You've warmed the cockles of an old woman's heart. Now run along, and I'll fix the coffee for you."

"She sure talks a lot, doesn't she?" Cynthia said. "She embarrasses me at times when she speaks out so frankly."

"I like her," Colter said. "She's a good woman, and she misses her husband very much."

Cynthia studied his face in the faint light coming through the curtains. She liked what she saw. "Were you serious inside when you said you were promised to someone?"

Colter laughed and gave his head a light shake. "I don't know anyone who would have me."

"I do," she answered.

"Who?"

"Mrs. O'Reilly. She thinks you're a fine-looking man who needs himself a good wife."

"What do you think?"

She sat silent for a while letting the swing rock gently to and fro. "I think she's right," she answered finally.

"On which part of the statement?"

"Both parts," she said, turning to face him. Her movement brought their hands together. He put his hand on hers and felt her grip tighten on his fingers.

"Here's the coffee," Mrs. O'Reilly said, setting a tray down on a small stand near the swing. "If you want anything else, just give a holler. I'll be inside."

"Thank you," they both said.

Colter sipped the coffee and tasted the good Irish whiskey inside. "That woman sure knows her way to a man's heart."

"I'll have to take lessons," Cynthia said.

Colter grinned. "You need no lessons, lassie," he

said, imitating Mrs. O'Reilly's brogue. "You've got ever'thing a man could possibly desire."

"Why, thank you, kind sir," Cynthia replied, keeping the tone light and hoping he hadn't heard her pounding heart.

They sat for a while holding hands, not saying anything. Then Colter broke the silence.

"Would you help me do something?"

"What?"

"I want you to say something to Sheridan Mason in front of Alcott, but I want it to look like a casual remark, like you don't feel that Alcott could possibly be interested in anything you're saying. Will you do that?"

"Certainly, but why?"

"If Alcott took the box and the letter that Jack wanted me to have, this will send him running to his partner. Then there won't be any doubt about his involvement."

"When do you want me to do this?"

"Tomorrow morning."

"All right. What do I say?"

"Tell Sheridan that you heard me say something about Jack being murdered over a big mining scheme. Tell him that I think I now know who killed my brother."

"That's all?"

"That's enough. If Alcott's guilty, he'll take off like a scared rabbit." He rose. "I'd better be going. I'll send Sheridan around about ten-thirty in the morning. Make sure Alcott's close enough to hear what you say, then watch what he does. Thank you for a great evening and a wonderful meal."

"Thank Mrs. O'Reilly for the food. I'm glad you could come, and I'm glad you enjoyed . . . everything."

He pulled her close. Her head tilted back and her

lips parted slightly in anticipation. He kissed her, and she clung to him for a moment, then pulled away. It wasn't that she didn't want to stay in his arms, it was for her own protection that she did it. She didn't trust herself. It had felt too good, and that worried her a little.

He said good night and headed back to his hotel room. Chirtua, Jack's old Indian drinking companion, was waiting for him in the darkness at the side of the hotel.

"Colter!"

Colter's hand dropped to the butt of his gun. "Who is it? Chirtua?"

"You have good ear for voice. I see same horse as last night—grulla with Bar K brand on hip."

"Where and when?"

Just then several riders turned the corner near the hotel and rode past the entrance. The one nearest Colter was John Kittleman, the other riders were Duke and the thin wrangler that Amos had called McQueen.

"You see grulla?"

Colter nodded. "Yes, McQueen was on him." It didn't make sense that McQueen would try to bushwhack him in a dark alley at night. He had only heard the man's name that afternoon. "Are you sure that's the same horse you saw the other night behind the store?"

"No make mistake. Same horse."

Colter dug a dollar from his pocket. "Here, Chirtua, have a drink on me. You've done well tonight." The old man accepted the coin, flashed a snaggle-toothed grin, and left.

This new revelation added nothing but confusion to Colter's mind. From the looks of it, he had figured Kittleman wrong from the beginning. Amos had him pegged for the kind of man he really was. Maybe Alcott would help clear up some of the confusion by leading Colter to the mysterious Mr. Stull. He would see in the morning.

The day broke as a gloomy one. An angry wind slapped shutters against the sides of buildings and hurled bits of stinging sand down the main street, causing the women shoppers to clutch their bonnets with a firm grip and walk with one shoulder forward. Colter stood where he could get protection from the blast but still be able to see the entrance of Duncan's Livery Stable in case Alcott decided to use the store's back door as an exit.

Sheridan Mason arrived on time, acknowledged Colter's presence with a nod, and went inside. After he had walked around for a bit looking at merchandise, he glanced at Cynthia. She shrugged and gestured with her hands to let him know that Alcott was not around. At that moment Alcott emerged from the back room and spotted Mason.

"Hello, Sheridan. What can I do for you?"

"Nothing right now. I was kind of hoping this pretty young lady here would wait on me."

Alcott laughed. "I can take a hint. I know when I'm not wanted."

Cynthia hurried over before Alcott left. "Good morning, Mr. Mason. What would you like?"

"That's a dangerous thing to ask an old man," he said, grinning, "but I'll settle for some tobacco."

She smiled. "By the way, I may have some news for your paper. Mr. Haines . . . you know, Jack's brother?" Sheridan nodded. "He said he thinks Jack was mixed up in some kind of mining scheme and that he was murdered because he may have known too much."

She glanced toward Alcott, who was pretending to be working at the counter but who was straining to catch every word.

"Mr. Haines said that he thinks he knows who Jack's killer is. Maybe you should talk to him. Sounds like a good story for your newspaper."

Sheridan smiled. "Maybe I should hire you as a reporter."

She smiled in return. "I doubt that I'd be much good."

Hank Alcott picked up something from a shelf and crammed it into a paper sack. Turning to Cynthia, he said, "Mrs. Henry forgot her thread. I'll just drive by and drop it off. I won't be long." He hurried out the front door and headed for Duncan's Livery Stable.

Colter watched Alcott lean into the wind as he turned the corner. Big splotches of rain began dropping, intermittently at first, and then became heavier as Colter reached for the slicker tied behind his saddle. Just after he had put it on and buttoned it, he saw Alcott come out of the stable and head down the street that led out of town. He followed at a discreet distance.

Alcott kept along the main road for a while and then cut across country in the direction of Kittleman's ranch. When he rode into the yard, he started to head for the bunkhouse, but Kittleman had heard him ride in and he called from the open door. "Who is it? That you, Alcott?" Alcott acknowledged that it was and Kittleman invited him in. "What in tarnation are you doin' ridin' out here on a day like this?"

Colter didn't hear the answer. He was busy tying his horse under a tree near the smokehouse. After the men had gone inside, Colter crept to the side of the house where he could watch what was going on without being seen. He couldn't hear much, only an occasional word.

Alcott brought the paper bag out of his pocket, retrieved the object he had put inside, and handed it to Kittleman. Kittleman smiled and called to his wife in a loud voice. In a few moments a slender gray-haired woman came into the room. She moved with difficulty and used two canes to help in her walking. Kittleman handed the object to her. She leaned one of the canes against her leg to free her hand and accepted Alcott's gift. There was genuine delight on her face as she examined it. It looked like a small perfume bottle made out of cut glass, Colter decided. Sarah Kittleman thanked Alcott for the gift. Then, after putting the bottle on the table, she admonished her husband for not offering Alcott a drink.

Alcott said something to Kittleman that caused him to yell for his Mexican servant. After a few words of instruction, the servant went out the door and returned a few minutes later with Duke. Kittleman excused himself and helped his wife back to their bedroom. While he was gone, Alcott took Duke by the arm and led him into the living room.

Colter started to move around to the other side of the house, but someone came out of the bunkhouse and he had to stop for fear of being seen.

Alcott told Duke everything he had heard. "What can be done about the situation?" he asked as worry crept into his voice.

"Why, hell, as far as I can see, we ain't got no choice," Duke said. "We've got to kill that damned cowboy before anybody finds out what he knows."

Colter had seen all he was going to see, so he untied his horse near the smokehouse and swung into the saddle. The cook, in the act of setting the garbage pail outside, saw Colter mount up and ride off. He thought it strange but said nothing about it until dinnertime.

Kittleman cursed him. "Why in the hell didn't you say something at the time? You know I don't like strangers poking around my house."

"I thought at first it was one of the hands. That's why I didn't say nothin'. Then, the more I thought about it, the more I knowed that wasn't a Bar K horse he was ridin'.''

"What kind was it?" Duke asked.

"It was a roan, a big one, and the feller ridin' it wasn't no slouch neither," the cook answered.

"It was Colter Haines," Duke said.

"Haines?" Kittleman asked. "What in the hell would he be sneakin' around here for?"

"I reckon he still figures you killed his brother," Duke said. As he said it, a scheme began to form in his mind. It brought a smile inside where no one could enjoy it but him. He had an answer to the problem Alcott had presented him with and one that would pay off handsomely if he worked it out right.

11

When Colter got back into town, he went to see Sheridan Mason at his office.

"Well," Colter said when he had finished his story, "what do you think?"

"I think you haven't got anything to build your case on."

"You saw what Alcott did when he swallowed the story Cynthia told you."

"Sure," Sheridan answered. "He put something into a bag and rode out to Kittleman's place to give Sarah Kittleman a present."

"You know that's a pile of horse manure."

"Certainly," Sheridan said. "You know it, and I know it, but no one else would, based on the 'evidence' you've just given me. Could you hear what they were saying to each other?"

"I've already told you I couldn't," Colter snapped.

"Precisely my point. It's pure conjecture on your part."

"What am I supposed to do, forget about the whole thing?"

Sheridan studied Colter's angry expression for several moments before he spoke. "It looks to me like you've got three alternatives: you can forget it, as you've just mentioned; you can try to get some evidence that'll hold up in court; or you can say the hell with evidence and shoot Alcott down like a dog. You'll have to make the choice yourself."

"What good would evidence against Alcott and this Rupert Stull do as long as Thompson is sheriff? Kittleman's got him in his hind pocket," Colter said.

"Don't sell Bill Thompson short. He said if there was murder involved, and it could be proven, he'd lock up whoever needed to be put in jail, and I believe him. Come on and I'll buy you a drink. You look like you need one."

As they were crossing the street heading toward Bascomb's, Levi Ormand spotted them and called to Colter. He came up to where the two men stood on the boardwalk waiting, and his face was beaming.

"You look like a cat that just swallowed a prairie chicken, Levi. What are you so all-fired happy about? You just get a contract to take care of all the army's guns or something?"

"Well, this young man asked me a question a couple of days ago, and I said if I could remember the answer, I'd tell him. I can and I'm here to tell him that the fella I sold that box of .52-caliber shells to was John Kittleman's foreman, Duke."

"You're sure?" Colter asked.

"Positive! I saw them in town last night, him and Mr. Kittleman, and that's when I remembered."

"I'm much obliged, Mr. Ormand. Can I buy you a drink in the way of sayin' thanks?"

"Heavens, no. I never touch the stuff. Well, good day." He headed back toward his gunshop.

"What's Duke's last name?" Colter asked.

"I don't think I've ever heard it. Most men don't give you their last name unless they're going into business or unless they're farmers."

"I still haven't got Duke's part figured in this whole thing. I don't know whether he's in this as a partner to Alcott or whether he and Kittleman are in cahoots or what. It's my guess that he and Alcott are workin' together, judgin' from the way they were actin' out at the Bar K. Whatever they were talkin' about, they sure didn't want Kittleman to hear it.''

"You're guessing again," Sheridan said. ''Maybe they were just keeping their voices down so they wouldn't disturb Mrs. Kittleman. She's not a well woman, you know.''

"They were tryin' to keep whatever they were sayin' from reachin' John Kittleman's ears. They don't give a damn about his wife.''

"So what are you going to do? Give up? Get evidence? Or gun down Alcott and Duke and maybe Kittleman too for good measure?''

"I'll try to do it all legallike . . . if I can. Now come on and buy me that drink.''

After Colter had finished the drink Sheridan had bought for him, he went to the Cattlemen's Range Restaurant for a meal. Inside he noticed the tables were all full. One near the rear of the room had only a single diner sitting at it. Colter asked if the man minded company for dinner, and the answer was a no and a request that Colter join him. As Colter sat down, he suddenly realized that the man on the other side of the table was the land-office clerk who had given him the map of Jack's ranch. While he was waiting for his order to be taken, he started a conversation with the clerk.

"That map you sold me really turned out to be handy.''

"Map?'' The clerk looked at him quizzically. Then he remembered where he'd seen Colter before. ''Oh, yes, the old Haines ranch.''

"I saw a fella out there yesterday and I think it was the new owner. What does this fella Stull look like? Is he a big man? I'd say about six-three and weighs in the neighborhood of 240 pounds?''

"That definitely sounds like him," the clerk responded.

"Do they call him Duke?"

"I think that's what Mr. Alcott called him, but I'm not certain."

The waitress interrupted their discussion by her arrival. Solving the mystery of who Rupert Stull was, finally settled in his mind, Colter suddenly felt very hungry and consequently ordered a big steak. Now that he had the information, however, he wasn't sure what he could do with it to build a legal fence around Duke and Hank Alcott. He figured the best thing to do would be to throw a scare into Alcott. Getting to Duke would be difficult unless he just happened to ride into town by himself. Going out to the Bar K to have it out with him was out of the question. He decided Alcott was the best bet.

Duke waited until darkness had lain over the Bar K spread for a good hour before he took his .52-caliber Spencer and sneaked out by the smokehouse. It was another half-hour wait until Sarah Kittleman joined her husband at the table for dinner. He raised the rifle and braced it against the corner of the building. Taking slow deliberate aim, he framed Sarah in his sights and waited until John Kittleman had seated his wife and started to pass by her to take his place on the opposite side of the table. At that moment, Duke squeezed the trigger and the heavy-caliber slug shattered the window and tore through Sarah Kittleman's chest and lightly grazed John's thigh as it buried itself in the log wall of the dining room.

Duke took off in a dead run around the rear of the main house and cut in between the cook's shack and the bunkhouse just as several of the men emerged to find out what the shooting was about.

"Curly Bill, you and Joe saddle up and see if you

can catch the jasper that fired that shot. The rest of you get your horses and wait. I'm gonna check on the boss and see if he's okay. He may want to do some ridin'.''

"Which way do we go?" Joe called as they headed for the corral.

"He took off north of the smokehouse," Duke answered. He then turned and ran to the house and pounded on the front door. "You all right, Mr. Kittleman?" Receiving no answer, he opened the door and burst into the room.

John Kittleman was kneeling on the rug in the dining room with his arms around Sarah's shoulders, gently rocking her back and forth. He had a stream of unashamed tears rolling down his cheeks. He kept repeating her name over and over again. "Sarah . . . Sarah . . . Sarah. Oh, God . . . oh, God. . .''

Duke clumped up next to him and stood for a moment looking down at Sarah's face. Death had drained her already pale coloring to a stark white. The front of her dress was bloody, but the floor contained an enormous amount that had spilled out of the jagged hole his bullet had torn in her back as it exited. He had shot other men before, but he'd never shot a woman, let alone seen one with a large piece of her back blown away. The sight brought a temporary flutter to his stomach.

Kittleman looked up at him, his face quivering with rage. "Who in the hell would shoot a woman who's never harmed a soul?"

"It was a big man on a roan. I just got a glimpse of him," Duke lied.

"Colter!" Kittleman said. "Have the boys saddle up. We're gonna catch that son of a bitch and hang him from the first tree we find. Send somebody in to get Doc Thatcher. There ain't nothin' he can do for her, but at least he can take her into town. Have him notify Bill Thompson. We don't need a sheriff for what I've got in mind, but it'll make it look legal.''

"Yes, sir!'' Duke said. "You able to ride with that leg wound?''

"I can ride. Why would he shoot Sarah, Duke? She was the kindest person I've ever known.''

"From the looks of things, I'd say he was tryin' to get you but missed his shot.''

"Let's ride. I'll be with you as soon as I put something on this leg.''

Colter finished his dinner and his conversation with the land-office clerk. Then rising, he said good night, paid his bill, and left. As he walked down the boardwalk, his thoughts turned to Cynthia. Within a few minutes he found himself outside Mrs. O'Reilly's house. The jovial Irishwoman answered his knock.

"Well, now, if it isn't himself come to call on young Miss Dobbs.''

Colter grinned. "Is she home?''

"And where else would a young lady of good breedin' be at this hour of the night, I ask you? Come in, come in, and I'll get the sweet thing for you.''

Colter followed her into the living room and stood by the fireplace looking at Mrs. O'Reilly's collection of photographs that were displayed on the mantel. Most of them were of her husband, Sean, in military uniform. He had been a colonel in the Union army serving under Sherman. There was one of him waving from a stretcher, a gift from the famous photographer Matthew Brady. Another showed him in the saddle on a magnificent gray gelding. He looked to be quite a man, and strong enough to have lived a long life enjoying Mrs. O'Reilly's fine cooking if the wound he'd received hadn't caused a lingering illness that finally resulted in his death.

Cynthia followed Mrs. O'Reilly into the room. She smiled broadly as Colter turned to greet her.

"Would you care for a cup of Irish coffee before I take my leave?" Mrs. O'Reilly asked.

"No, thanks," Colter replied. "I just finished eating dinner. You don't have to leave, though, Mrs. O'Reilly. I've come to ask Cynthia out for a walk."

Cynthia turned back toward her room. "I'll get a wrap and be with you in a moment."

Colter nodded toward the photographs. "He looked to be a real figure of a man."

"He was, God rest his soul. No better man ever trod the face of the earth. 'Twas a loss for me and all that knew him. You remind me of him in some ways."

Before Mrs. O'Reilly could speak on her thoughts, Cynthia returned with a shawl over her shoulders.

"Shall we go?"

Colter took her arm and then said good night to Mrs. O'Reilly.

When they were outside, Cynthia asked, "What were you two talking about? You both looked so serious when I returned."

"Her husband. He was a fine-looking man, strong and well-set-up. Well, speaking of fine-looking, you certainly fill the bill, young lady."

She smiled. "Is this just a social call or did you have something to talk about that's important?"

"Now, would I spoil a nice evening stroll with a beautiful woman by talking business? Don't answer that. There are a couple of things I want to tell, but they can wait awhile." He took her arm and they walked slowly toward the outskirts of town talking about everything in general and nothing in particular. When they had strolled for about an hour, they turned and headed back toward town. A rider passed them at a dead run.

"I wonder what's so all-fired important that makes him run his horse like that?"

"Maybe there's trouble somewheres," Cynthia answered. "There always seems to be something going on lately."

A few minutes later, Colter could hear a big group of riders coming their way. He took Cynthia's arm and guided her off the main road. They watched as Sheriff Thompson and ten men rode past in the dark.

"That looks like a posse," Colter commented. As they started back toward the road, he heard another horse coming, but this one was pulling a buckboard. It was Doc Thatcher. "Looks like somebody got shot up."

"We'll find out when we get back to town," she said.

When they reached the outermost buildings, they could see people in the streets, which was unusual for this time of night. Sounds of excited talking drifted in the night air. Cynthia touched Colter's arm, and they stopped when they heard someone spreading the story.

"They said he shot her right through the window, killing her and wounding Mr. Kittleman with the same bullet."

"Who done the shootin'?"

"That Haines fella, the brother of the one that was killed a couple of months ago."

"When did it happen?"

" 'Bout an hour ago, I guess."

"Well, I hope they string him up good. We don't need his kind around here. Any man that would shoot a woman. . ." The voices drifted off again.

"That's crazy!" Cynthia exclaimed. "You've been with me for over an hour."

"Somebody's tryin' to set me up for a hangin', and I think I know who."

"What are you going to do, Colter?"

"Stay away from town till I can find a way to catch the guy that set me up and prove that I didn't shoot Sarah Kittleman."

"Don't you think it would be wiser to turn yourself in to Sheriff Thompson. After all, I can vouch that you were with me for the last hour and a half, and it's a good half-hour ride from here to Kittleman's ranch. That would mean she would have to have been shot at least two hours ago. The man said she was killed a little over an hour ago. That should prove your innocence."

"It doesn't prove anything. They'd say you were making up the story to protect me."

"Where will you go? What will you do?"

"I don't know yet, but I'd better get out of town before Thompson gets back. I'll keep in touch."

She took his arm. "When will I see you again?"

"I can't say right now."

She moved closer. "I'm worried."

As she looked up at him, he took her shoulders and pulled her toward him. She yielded and parted her lips slightly in anticipation. He kissed her hard and passionately. There was an urgency flowing from him that she could feel, an excitement that the situation had brought on partially, but the rest of it, she sensed, was because of their bodies clinging together so closely.

He turned without a word and walked toward the livery stable.

Kittleman saw the posse coming toward him as the moon poked its bare face through a hole in the big cumulus cloud above. He called his men to a halt and waited.

Sheriff Thompson drew to a stop as he met the Bar K riders. "Where are you headed, Mr. Kittleman?"

"We were going to town to find Colter Haines."

"What makes you so sure it was Haines that shot Sarah?"

"Duke got a look at him."

The sheriff turned toward the burly foreman. "How positive were you that it was Colter Haines? Did you get a clear look?"

"I saw a big man on a roan leaving from behind the smokehouse right after I heard the shot."

"A big man on a roan," Thompson repeated. "What time was this? About an hour ago?"

"What in the hell difference does it make, Bill?" Kittleman growled. "He saw him and that's good enough. We're wastin' time."

"What time, Duke?" the sheriff repeated.

"We were just sittin' down to dinner," Kittleman said angrily. "Sarah liked to eat at eight P.M.. You could set your watch by it."

"How could you tell it was a roan in the dark?" the sheriff continued pressing in.

Duke shifted uncomfortably in the saddle. "The moonlight caught him just as he mounted up," he said. "If we don't get goin', Mr. Kittleman, he could be halfway to Colorado before we catch up."

"All right, men, let's ride!" Kittleman shouted.

"Hold it!" Thompson's voice thundered. "I've got a sworn-in posse with me, and we'll do the catchin'. You're welcome to come along if you wish, but there'll be no lynchin' party. If we get him, he goes back to town to stand trial."

"Like hell he does!" Kittleman snarled. "When we get him, we hang him. If you try to stop us, I'll kill you."

"Kittleman," the sheriff said. It was the first time he had ever addressed John Kittleman without the customary "Mr." in front of his name, and Kittleman's eyes narrowed in anger at the obvious lack of humility on Bill Thompson's part. "You put me in as sheriff to see that law and order were carried out. I admit that it was mainly your interpretation of law and order that I upheld, but that ain't the way it is anymore. Too many questions have come up recently that don't have clear answers to them.''

"I don't know what in the hell you're talkin' about, Sheriff, but as far as I'm concerned, you're fired. Come on, boys.''

"He's not in town. I just came from there," Thompson said.

"He's prob'bly hidin' out at the sheepherder's place," Duke said. "That's where he stayed when Yeager shot him.''

"Let's go!" Kittleman said.

The Bar K riders turned and followed their boss as he and Duke headed north. Thompson and his posse swung in behind them.

Amos sat smoking his pipe in front of the fireplace and watching Johnny feed the little lamb that had become an orphan when Duke had shot its mother.

"Won't be long 'fore that little feller can handle life on his own, Johnny. You done a good job takin' care of him. I believe he's a mite bigger and stronger than them that still have their mothers."

"Yeah," Johnny said. "He's a big 'un."

Amos leaned forward and listened as the thundering sound of a large group of riders came through the open window. He grabbed his shotgun and opened the door just as they reined to a halt in front of his cabin.

Kittleman spoke. "Is Colter Haines here?"

"Maybe he is and maybe he ain't," Amos countered. "What's it to you?"

Kittleman glanced at Duke and nodded toward Amos. Duke dismounted and walked toward the old man. Amos swung the barrel of his shotgun up, but Duke drew and fired, hitting him in the left arm. Amos tried lifting the gun again, but Duke hit him in the face and knocked him to the ground. After Amos had fallen, Duke stepped into the cabin.

Johnny looked up from where he knelt beside the lamb. "Yore the one who shot his momma."

Duke grinned. "That's right, dummy. I just shot your pa too, and I'll shoot you if you don't tell me where Colter Haines is."

"Yeah . . . Colter," Johnny repeated.

Duke kicked Johnny hard in the side, sending him falling over the little lamb. It bleated in fright. Duke leaned over and grabbed Johnny by the shirt and pulled him to his feet. "Now, stupid, where's Colter gone to?"

Johnny held his side and gasped for air.

"Did you hear me, dummy? Where's Colter Haines?"

Johnny looked at Duke bewildered. "Colter's a nice man. He don't hurt people."

Duke hit Johnny full in the face and knocked him to the floor, where he lay in an unconscious heap.

"Duke!" Kittleman called.

Duke stepped out of the door. "He ain't here, Mr. Kittleman."

"What did you do to my boy?" Amos said, struggling to his feet.

"Taught him some manners," Duke replied, grinning.

"The next time you or any of yore slop-eatin', asskissin', backshootin' crew come on to my land, Kittleman, I'll kill you and ever' goddamned one of you that trespasses. Now git off my land or by God I'll blast you where you sit." He cocked both barrels of the shotgun. "Why don't you try drawin' on me now, Duke, you lard-ass son of a bitch?"

Duke just grinned and wheeled his horse around as the group headed out of the yard.

Amos eased both hammers back to the safe position and staggered into the house. Johnny was just beginning to regain consciousness, and he was bleeding from the cut on his lip where Duke had hit him. Amos' face softened as he watched Johnny sit up.

"What did I do, Pa?" His voice was filled with bewilderment.

"You didn't do nothin' wrong, son. They was just a mean bunch of bastards, that's all. Put some water in that pot on the stove, then help me tear this sleeve off. I'll clean you up in a jiffy."

"Yeah . . . in a jiffy," Johnny said as he poured water in the pot.

12

Colter moved the roan into the trees as the big group of riders came to the crossroads nearby. They stopped to talk, and he could hear them clearly. They were arguing.

"I told you you were fired!" Kittleman shouted.

"You can't fire me," Thompson replied. "It has to be done by the city council."

"That'll be taken care of first thing in the morning."

"Until then, by God, I'm still sheriff. If that old man wants to press charges against you for trespassin' and against Duke for assault, I'll lock you both up. Now I'm tellin' you for the last time, go home and leave the law work to me."

"I'll take care of you tomorrow, Thompson. Let's go, boys."

Colter thought about Thompson's words. The old man he mentioned had to be Amos. He turned the roan in the direction of Amos' cabin and nudged it in the flank. As he rode into the yard, he saw the light go out, and he heard Amos bellow.

"Sing out or I'll drop you!"

Colter grinned. "It's me, Amos. Colter Haines."

The door opened and Amos' shaggy head protruded. "Well, I'll be dogged. Bring that light here, Johnny, then go take care of Colter's horse. We got comp'ny.

Come in, Colter. Just had some fellers here a-lookin' for you.''

Colter dismounted and handed the reins to Johnny. He noticed Johnny's cut face. "How you doin', Johnny?''

"It's him, Pa. It's Colter.''

"Yeah, it's him. Now take care of his horse. Come in, Colter, before those backshooters show up again and blow you all to hell.''

Amos explained how Duke had shot him and mistreated Johnny.

Colter sat seething in anger. "If there was ever a man that needed killin', it's Duke.''

"If you've got some reason for shootin' him, you can git in line right behind me,'' Amos said. "By the way, why were they lookin' for you? You send another of Kittleman's boys to boot hill?''

"Nope. It was his wife Sarah.''

Amos started to chuckle but stopped and studied Colter's face carefully. "You sayin' John Kittleman's wife is dead, or are you joshin' me?''

"No, she's dead, all right, and I'm supposed to have killed her.''

"Who's doin' all this accusin' anyways?''

"Your fat friend Duke. He says he saw me shoot Mrs. Kittleman through their window just as John and his missus were sittin' down to eat their dinner.''

"Why that slop-eatin', egg-suckin', lyin' son of a bitch. He prob'bly done it hisself. Where was you when all this was a-goin' on?''

"I was either havin' dinner with the clerk from the land office, or I was out walkin' Cynthia Dobbs.''

"Then you ain't got nothin' to worry about. You got yoreself one of them alleybys.''

"I don't think Kittleman would take the time to listen. I think he wants to hang first and talk later.''

"You reckon the sheriff would help you out if you was to tell him what you just told me?"

"I don't know if he's goin' to be in a position to help anybody, come mornin'. I heard him and Kittleman havin' some words on the road out here. He threatened to take Kittleman to jail if he didn't turn around and head back to the Bar K and take his men with him, seein' as how they had a hangin' in mind instead of justice."

"The hell you say! How did Kittleman take to havin' his own appointed sheriff suddenly snappin' at the hand that feeds him?"

"He didn't like it, and he told the sheriff he'd be out of office the first thing tomorrow mornin'."

"Well, I'll be jiggered. I guess maybe I been judgin' that sheriff with the wrong set of measurements."

Colter grinned. "The sheriff also said that if you wanted to press charges against Duke for assault, he'd go out to Kittleman's spread and bring old fat gut in to jail."

"By God, I've got a good mind to do that. I prob'-bly would too if the sheriff had a decent deputy workin' for him. Kittleman's such a low-down sidewinder, he'd most likely shoot the sheriff for tryin' to uphold the law. I don't want nobody blowed apart on my account. Besides, I'd like to ventilate Duke my own self."

Johnny came in grinning. "I done his horse, Pa."

"You did, huh? Well, let's see how good you are at pourin' some coffee for Colter and me. You too if you want some."

"Yeah! Coffee for Colter." Johnny stopped for a minute and blinked several times. He liked the sound of the words he'd just said. He grinned and said them in reverse. "Colter and coffee. Colter and coffee, Pa." He was proud of the words. It was the closest he had ever come to forming anything poetic.

"Sounds kinda musical, don't it?" Amos said to him.

Johnny laughed and repeated the words several more times as he poured coffee into three cups.

Turning his attention to Colter once more, Amos asked, "So what are you gonna do, give yoreself up when things cool down, or try to git a-hold of Duke and make him talk, or what?"

"I'll try to talk to the sheriff in the mornin'. That is, *if* he's still in office. I've got to get in and talk to your friend Sheridan. He's on the town council and I think he should argue against Sheriff Thompson bein' fired by Kittleman. I also need to throw a scare into Alcott. I don't believe he'll have much backbone if I get him alone and let him know I'm onto his little scheme."

"I don't thank you'll have to light a fire under Sheridan. He'll argue against Kittleman just to see the sparks fly."

"Maybe I'd better see Alcott tonight. He's also on the town council, and he'll swing along with Kittleman unless I convince him to do otherwise. It might be wise to see the sheriff tonight too. It'll give him more information to back himself up with at the council meeting tomorrow." He rose and put on his hat. "That was good coffee, Johnny. If I don't get thrown in jail, maybe I'll ride out tomorrow afternoon and have another cup. Good-bye, Amos." He stepped to the door and paused. "You want me to send Doc Thatcher out to have a look at that arm?"

"Yeah, why don't you do that? I'll have him add it to Kittleman's bill. That sidewinder ought to pay for somethin'. Johnny, go fetch Colter's horse for him."

Johnny took off running and in a few minutes returned leading Colter's horse. It was saddled and ready to ride.

Colter shook hands, said his good-byes, and rode

back to town. He had decided to see Alcott first, so he rode around the edge of town and stopped at the back door of the store owner's house. He peered cautiously through a window and saw Alcott checking some figures in a ledger book. Testing the rear door and finding it unlocked, he eased himself inside and made his way to the kitchen, where he could see Alcott working at his desk in the living room. He drew his .45 and started to step into the room when he was halted by a knock at the front door.

Alcott rose and called, "Who is it?"

"It's Bill Thompson, Hank. I'd like to talk to you about something important."

Alcott opened the door and let the sheriff in. "What's the problem?"

"Hank, I'm going to need a few friendly votes tomorrow from the town council."

"Whatever for?"

"I guess you haven't heard. You knew that Sarah Kittleman was shot and killed this evening, didn't you?"

"Yes, I heard some folks talking about it on my way home from the store. A real tragedy, but what has this got to do with council votes?"

"John Kittleman wants to catch Colter Haines and lynch him. He's not interested in having me uphold the law. I formed a posse tonight, and we looked for Haines. We met Kittleman and his Bar K riders out on a little vigilante trip into town. When I told him Haines wasn't in town, Duke suggested that we ride out to that old sheepherder's place. When we got there Duke shot the old man because he was trying to prevent us from trespassing, which Carson had every right to do. Then, when Duke didn't find Haines in the old man's shack, Kittleman was fit to be tied. I told him to go home, take his boys with him, and leave the legal work to me and my deputized posse. He said I was fired. I told him that was an action only the town council could do. He said he'd take care of *that* first thing in the morning.''

''If I was in Kittleman's shoes, I'd want Colter Haines strung from the nearest tree same as he does.''

Sheriff Thompson studied Hank's face. ''Since I got back to town, I had a visit from your clerk, Cynthia Dobbs. She informed me that Colter Haines was with her at the time Duke claims to have seen a big man on a roan riding away just after the shot was fired.''

''I'd believe Duke before I would that girl. It seems kind of obvious that she's quite taken with the man and hopes to save him by lying.''

''It's just as obvious that Duke hates the man and hopes to have him caught and hanged, and he's not above lying to accomplish just that.''

''You'd better not let Duke hear you call him a liar. He wouldn't take kindly to that.''

Sheriff Thompson ignored Alcott's comment and continued, ''There's no way Duke could have seen the color of a horse at that hour of the evening. Kittleman gave me the time of the shooting, and it doesn't add up. The moon didn't rise until thirty minutes after Sarah was shot. Besides, Cynthia's landlady, Mrs. O'Reilly, confirmed the fact that Colter Haines was at her house a few minutes before the shooting took place.

''So you want me to vote against John Kittleman. Is that it?''

''Yes, that's it.''

''I can't. Kittleman's Bar K Ranch brings me more business than anything else in this part of the country. I'd be cutting my own throat if I did that.''

Sheriff Thompson snorted in disgust. ''Don't you ever think of anything besides money? What about a man's life? If they catch Haines, they'll string him up unless I'm there to stop them. Do you want that on your conscience, the hanging of an innocent man?''

''I don't give a damn about Colter Haines. He's nothing but a troublemaker, just like Jack was. This community would be a lot better off without him around.''

''You mean maybe you and Duke and a few others would be better off without him around.''

Hank Alcott's eyes narrowed suspiciously. ''What do you mean by that remark?''

''Colter's onto something, and it has to do with Jack's murder. I wouldn't be surprised if he pays you a visit some night.''

''Jack's murder? Everyone knows he was killed by Kramer.'' Alcott's voice quivered.

''Everyone *thinks* he was killed by Kramer. Everyone except Colter and me and Sheridan Mason, and I don't know how many others. Good night, Hank. I hope you sleep well.''

Hank Alcott stood dumbfounded in the center of the room for several minutes after Thompson left. Then, after checking to make sure the sheriff was gone, he locked the door and went back to his desk. He unlocked a lower drawer and extracted a metal box. From the inside, he took out a letter and began to read it. He had read it before, the day he'd found it in the store where Cynthia had placed it, but he wanted to check again just to make certain that there was reason enough to kill to keep it out of unwanted hands.

''Do you always read other people's mail?''

Alcott gave a short gasp of fear and then whirled around to find himself staring right into the barrel of Colter's .45.

''What . . . How did you get in here?''

Colter ignored the question. ''I'll take my letter now *and* the box.'' Hank handed him the letter Jack had written. In handing him the box, a fleeting thought of throwing it and trying to grab a gun from his desk passed through Hank's mind, but Colter read his action. "I wouldn't advise trying anything dumb, Mr. Alcott. I won't put a bullet in your back like you did Jack's. I'll just blow your head off."

"I didn't kill Jack."

"It was either you or Duke. It doesn't make much difference to me either way. I'm gonna shoot both of you anyhow." He cocked his gun.

"Wait! Duke did it. He shot your brother just after Jack found out about the copper ore. Then, he killed Kramer to make it look like they'd shot each other following an argument."

"Did Duke know about the copper at that time?"

"No, he shot Jack because he thought your brother was getting too close to the Kittlemans and that Jack would eventually take over the ranch. Sarah Kittleman thought Jack looked like her son, and she loved to have him visit 'cause he'd take her out on buggy rides. Those were the only times she ever got out of the house."

"I thought John Kittleman didn't like Jack."

"At first he did like Jack, but then Duke started telling John that Jack was just trying to worm his way in on the good side of Sarah so that he might inherit the Bar K."

"The Bar K belongs to John, doesn't it?"

"It belonged to Sarah, actually. It was her money that bought the land and the cattle. She had a strong hand in running the ranch till her young son died in that fire. Then, she got sick and started having problems walking. That's when John took over."

"And started running the homesteaders out. When did Duke enter the picture?"

"He was kind of an adopted son. The Kittlemans took him in when his folks died of smallpox. He was only about fifteen then. He's been with the Bar K for twenty years that I know of."

"So he's hoping to inherit the ranch himself, isn't he?"

Alcott's expression was contemplative. "I hadn't really thought about it, but it makes sense."

"How did you get involved in this?"

"Jack brought some of the malachite in to me to ask about it. I knew it was loaded with copper, but I didn't know where he'd gotten it. I told him what it was. That's when he wrote you that letter and filled that box with copper ore. I was on my way out to see Jack when Duke shot him. That's when I told Duke about the ore. We rode around Jack's place until we found the vein. When we discovered that it crossed Kramer's place before turning onto Bar K property, Duke got the idea of killing Kramer and then he and I would buy up the two ranches."

"Only he didn't buy Jack's ranch. He forged Jack's name on the deed. Was he going to tell Kittleman about the copper?"

"I don't know. Maybe he wanted to wait until he found out how he stood on inheriting the Bar K."

"He didn't wait very long. I think he killed Sarah Kittleman so that John would go after me. He probably figured I'd kill John first if we tangled with each other. That would leave the Bar K without any heirs except maybe Duke. I wouldn't even be surprised if it was Duke that burned Fernley's cabin fifteen years ago, killing the Kittleman's only son and heir. It's certainly his style."

"My God!" Alcott exclaimed. "If that's true, it means that Duke has killed eight or nine innocent people, if you include the Fernley family. How could I have gotten mixed up with such a man?"

"Greed, I believe, is the term. Duke might make

you number ten if he feels that he can profit from your death.''

Alcott swallowed with difficulty because of a throat dried out by fear. ''Oh, God! I never thought of that. Do you suppose he would?''

''A man that would calmly shoot a woman that was a second mother to him just as she's sitting down to eat is capable of anything.''

''What can I do?''

''I think you're safe tonight, but you'll have to testify against Duke in court on my brother's death and on the Kramer killing.''

''He'll kill me for sure if I do that.''

''Not if Bill Thompson is still sheriff. Remember that tomorrow at the council meeting. He needs your vote.''

''Will I have to go to jail?''

''That's up to the sheriff. I'm leaving now, but I'll be around, so don't try and double-cross me.'' He tucked the box under his arm and went out the back door. He heard Alcott turn the key in the lock as he mounted up.

13

Colter rode down the back streets until he reached Duncan's Livery Stable. He knocked on the door, but the stablehand was gone and no one was inside. He took his roan in and unsaddled it. After rubbing it down with a rag he found hanging from a nail, he turned the horse into one of the empty stalls and gave it a good helping of oats. Then, he headed for the hotel.

When he entered the lobby, he found the night clerk asleep in a chair behind the desk. Rather than cause any alarm, he let the clerk continue to sleep and took the key to number ten from the pigeonhole behind the counter. He let himself into his room and pulled the curtains together. He was tired, and he wanted no early-morning sunbeams hitting him in the eyes. Things had cleared up enormously tonight, and tomorrow might see the end of all his troubles. A good night's rest would put everything in its proper perspective. He took off his gun belt, his boots, and his hat, and stretched out on the top blanket. He feel asleep immediately.

Sheriff Thompson stood at the counter of the Imperial Hotel glaring at the clerk. "What in the hell do you mean, he didn't come in? His horse is in the livery stable. Is his key in the box?"

"Yes," the clerk said indignantly, "it's right here in number . . . It's gone!"

"Of course it's gone, you idiot. If you hadn't been sleeping on duty, you'd have known he was upstairs."

"But, Sheriff, he must have come in while. . ." His argument was lost on Thompson because the sheriff had bounded up the stairs two at a time and now stood outside number ten with his gun drawn. He tried the knob and the door was unlocked. Cautiously pushing the door inward, he tiptoed to the edge of the bed and picked up Colter's .45 and gun belt where it hung from the back of a chair.

"All right, Haines, on your feet!"

Colter awoke and automatically reached for his gun, only to discover that Bill Thompson held it in his left hand. His eyes narrowed.

"What's the idea, Sheriff?"

"I'm taking you in for murder."

"You know damned well I didn't kill Sarah Kittleman."

"I'm not talking about Sarah Kittleman. I'm taking you in for killing Hank Alcott."

"Hank Alcott? I talked to him last night and I left him in good health."

"You were the last one to see him alive. Mrs. Hanley, his neighbor, said she saw you sneaking out the back door in the dark. She said you got on your horse and rode out of town."

"I didn't ride *out* of town. I rode to the other side, so I could enter Duncan's stable from the rear door. When was Alcott shot?"

"Who said he was shot?"

"That's the way a man is usually killed in this part of the country unless it's an Apache arrow. Did he have a feathered shaft in his back?"

"You'd know that better than I would. Get your boots on. We're going to jail."

Colter put his hat on, pulled on his boots, and walked out the door, followed by Thompson with a drawn gun.

The town-council meeting convened at nine A.M. by special demand of John Kittleman. He was red-eyed and haggard-looking from the loss of his wife and from having spent most of the night drinking and getting very little sleep. He was in no mood for argument, and his patience was nonexistent.

Sheriff Thompson was not present but had sent word that he would be a few minutes late. The delay was especially exasperating to Kittleman. He could see no reason for holding up the meeting to accommodate the sheriff. After all, it was the sheriff he had ridden in town to fire and a man didn't have to be present to be fired.

Sheridan Mason, Levi Ormand, the town banker Dean Edgerton, Judge Jay Gordon, Hank Alcott, John Kittleman and Jacob Haggerty the undertaker made up the seven-man council. Those alive and assembled persuaded Kittleman to wait citing the fact that it would only be fair to wait for Hank Alcott to arrive and to have the sheriff present to hear the charges brought against him.

Sheriff Thompson took Colter down a back street to the jail. As they walked, he listened while Colter outlined a scheme. "As long as you haven't told anyone that Hank Alcott is dead, why don't you just say that he was seriously wounded but is still alive. The only one that could or would have killed Alcott is Duke Stull. I had no reason to kill him. He told me everything I wanted to know. He also said that he would vote to keep you in your job."

"How'd you know about that?"

"I was in his house when you came in, only neither one of you knew it."

"What good will lying about Alcott's death do?"

"It'll bring the real killer, Duke, out of the woodwork. If you let on that Alcott is unconscious but that you hope to learn who shot him as soon as he wakes up, Duke will panic. He doesn't strike me as bein' particularly bright anyhow. You can say that you're keepin' Alcott in a cell here at the jail for his own protection. Duke will have to find some way of getting in here to kill Alcott before Alcott spills the beans. When he does, you can pick him up."

Thompson glanced at his watch. "I must be loco to listen to you. I'm already late for the council meeting."

"Another thing," Colter went on. "If you can, find the slug that killed Sarah Kittleman; you can bet me it's a fifty-two-caliber, and it came from a Spencer owned by Duke Stull. It'll match the one that just missed me when I was out riding over Jack's property."

"You're pretty certain about all this, aren't you?"

"If it doesn't add up, I give you my word I'll let you hang me for Alcott's murder."

Thompson grinned. "That's not much of a bargain. I've already got you on that charge."

"Oh, one more thing," Colter said, ignoring Thompson's comment. "When you see Doc Thatcher so he'll verify your story, tell him to ride out and take care of Amos' arm. Duke's bullet kinda tore it up a bit."

"You must be crazy if you think I'm going to ride out to John Kittleman's place to look for a bullet."

When they reached the rear of the jail, Thompson told Colter to take the path between the jail and the hardware store. Colter suddenly spun around and drove a fist into Thompson's jaw. The lawman dropped unconscious to the ground. Colter grabbed his gun and ran.

* * *

"Even though Hank Alcott is missing, I'm calling this council meeting to order," Dean Edgerton said. "Now, I'd like to . . . *we* would like to hear the reason for this emergency meeting, John."

"Bill Thompson is unfit to be the sheriff any longer. I want him out as of now."

"Why do you want him out, John?" Judge Gordon asked.

"Last night my wife was murdered, shot to death in her own living room by Colter Haines. My boys and I rode out to catch him, and we were ordered home by Thompson and threatened with arrest if we didn't go. There's not a man here that wouldn't have done exactly as I did, and then to be ordered home by the man you yourself put into office was just too much. A good sheriff would have ridden all night and he'd have had something to show for it this mornin'." He spun and faced Thompson angrily. "Have you got that killer Haines behind bars yet?"

"No," Thompson said quietly as he rubbed the sore spot on his jaw.

"See what I mean. The man's incompetent."

"I don't have Haines in jail because Haines didn't kill your wife."

Kittleman glared. "That's a lie! My foreman saw him mount up and ride away right after the shot was fired."

"I won't say Duke is a liar, I'll just say he was mistaken. First of all," Thompson said, turning to the rest of the councilmen, "at the time Sarah Kittleman was shot, it was pitch-dark outside. The moon didn't rise until at least half an hour later. Yet Duke said he saw a big man get on a roan and ride off. You can't tell a horse's color in the dark, let alone identify the man riding it. Second of all, Colter Haines was in town at the time of the shooting."

"I heard about that girl's story and it's obvious she's lying!" Kittleman shouted.

"Not only did he take Miss Cynthia Dobbs for a walk about that time," Thompson said, staring pointedly at Kittleman, "but he had dinner with Willie Furtch, the clerk in the land office."

Kittleman fell into sullen silence.

Thompson relaxed a bit and continued, "Mr. Kittleman would certainly have hung Colter Haines if he'd managed to catch him, and then I would have been duty-bound to take Mr. Kittleman to jail for murder."

"Then who did shoot Mrs. Kittleman if this Haines fella is innocent?" Dean Edgerton asked.

"I believe it was the same man that shot Hank Alcott," Thompson answered.

"Hank Alcott?" several councilmen said at the same time.

"When was Hank shot?" Sheridan asked.

"Sometime last night."

"Was he killed?"

"No, he's still alive," Thompson answered, "although he's unconscious. He was shot sometime around midnight, as near as I can figure. He should be able to tell who shot him just as soon as he wakes up. I'm keeping him in the jail for his own protection until I can learn the identity of the man that tried to kill him."

"I wondered why Hank wasn't here this morning," Levi Ormand commented.

"Well," Sheridan said, rising, "as far as I'm concerned, I think Bill Thompson is doing a damned good job, and I should think you'd be grateful to him for keeping you from hanging an innocent man, John, instead of trying to get him fired. How do the rest of you feel?"

One by one the councilmen agreed with Sheridan. Thompson would keep his job as sheriff. Kittleman turned without a further word and stormed out of the room.

Thompson thanked the men present for backing him, then turned and left. He needed to contact Doc Thatcher and he needed to make up a bunk in the jail so that it would look like it was occupied by an injured man. He cursed himself for being careless and letting Colter get the drop on him so easily. He blamed Colter's story for keeping his mind busy sorting out what he had been told. It was irritating to him, but he had to admit that Colter's scheme made sense. In fact, it made more sense to think of Duke as the murderer of both Sarah Kittleman and Hank Alcott than it did Colter.

Colter had nothing to gain by killing Sarah Kittleman. Duke, on the other hand, had good reason, considering the value of the Bar K Ranch and the fact that he was considered the closest thing to an heir that the Kittlemans had. Still, he would like to have kept Colter in jail until he had gotten everything sorted out. Colter must have known that he would not be chased until sometime after the town-council meeting. He must also have known that Thompson would not get a posse together because that might possibly be interpreted as another sign of incompetence. Thompson shook his head in disgust. That damned Haines was a little too sharp for his own good. One of these days it just might backfire on him.

14

.

John Kittleman rode into the yard in front of the Bar
K ranch house and dismounted. A Mexican wrangler
took the horse and led it to the corral to unsaddle it.
Kittleman stood for a while watching Duke draw a
map in the dirt with a stick so that he could point out
to all the hands that were present exactly which canyon
areas were likely to contain the most cattle.

The Mexican wrangler returned. "Anything else,
Señor Kittleman?"

"Yes, Carlos. Tell Duke I want to see him. I'll be
inside."

"Sí, señor."

Kittleman was pouring himself a drink when a knock
sounded on the thick oak door. "Come in," he called.

Duke entered. "What's up, boss? Did you get the
sheriff fired?"

Kittleman took a sip from his glass and stared at
Duke for several moments before he answered.

Duke began to feel a little uncomfortable under Kittleman's probing stare. "Is there somethin' wrong,
Mr. Kittleman?"

"Yeah, Duke. Bill Thompson pretty well made you
out to be a liar."

Duke's face clouded. "What'd he call me a liar
about?"

"The shooting last night. He said the moon hadn't

come up yet and that it was too dark to see the color of a horse.''

"I don't give a damn what he said," Duke countered. "I know what I saw. All right, so maybe I didn't see the color of the horse, but when you know the man that did the shootin', you just naturally assume that he rode the same horse he always rides. What in the hell difference does the color of the horse make anyhow? The horse didn't pull the trigger.''

"You're certain it was Colter Haines that fired the shot?''

"Dead certain!''

"That's good enough for me. Thompson seemed to imply that whoever it was that shot Sarah also shot Alcott.''

Duke's face twitched noticeably, but Kittleman had turned to refill his glass and missed it.

"Well, I'm sure that mystery will be cleared up as soon as Hank regains consciousness.''

"You mean he wasn't killed?'' Duke fought to keep the anxiety out of his voice.

"No, Thompson said he was keeping Hank in a jail cell for his own protection. I guess Hank will be able to say who shot him as soon as he wakes up.''

"Is there anything else you wanted to talk to me about, boss? I've got a lot of things lined up I'd better be lookin' after. I've got to go into town and see Haggerty.''

Kittleman squinted at his burly foreman. It was unlike Duke to want to leave before he'd been offered a drink. Oh, well, he thought, I did ask him to take care of the funeral arrangements. "No, I don't have anything else,'' he answered.

Duke muttered a "See you later'' and left.

Duke walked by the jail on his way back from Haggerty's Undertaking Parlor. He glanced in the window and saw no one at the sheriff's desk. Turning back to the hitching rail where he had left his horse, he mounted and rode around to the side window of the jail. Peering into the darkened interior, he spotted a figure lying on a bunk and covered by a sheet. He drew his gun, and after glancing over his shoulder to make sure no one was watching, he fired three quick shots through the window, then spurred his horse and galloped around the corner.

Bill Thompson stood at the bar in Bascomb's Saloon with his foot on the brass rail holding on to a half-empty glass of beer. He was troubled. Two murders in less than twenty-four hours and no real clues to go on. He'd sat around the jail for a while waiting to see if Colter's prediction about Duke Stull would come to pass. Duke hadn't shown up, and after four hours of drinking last night's warmed-over coffee, he'd had enough sitting. Besides, who knew if Colter's story was the right one or Duke's.

At the moment Duke had shot through the window, a loud burst of laughter had erupted from some cowboys telling a story in the rear of the bar, and it had drowned out the sound of gunfire. Thompson was unaware that it had happened, and so when Duke stopped in at Bascomb's for a beer and to establish an alibi, Thompson was surprised to see him. He had expected that if Duke did come into town to "kill" Hank Alcott, he would most likely shoot and run.

"What are you doing in town, Duke?"

Duke ordered a beer and stared at the sheriff for a few seconds before answering. "You pass a law against havin' a beer?"

Thompson straightened up. He didn't want to have a confrontation with Duke. He knew that Duke could take him physically and also beat him to the draw, but he didn't feel that his question should elicit such a hostile answer. "What in the hell's got into you? I asked a simple question and you sound like you're ready to knock my head off."

Duke realized that he was pushing it in the way he was responding, and he really didn't want to do that. It was just that Thompson was getting too close in his suspicions even though he probably wasn't aware of it.

"I guess I just ain't feeling too good about the killin' that's been goin' on. Sarah Kittleman was like a mother to me, and I had to come in today and make arrangements for puttin' her in the ground."

"When is the buryin'?"

"This afternoon at five-thirty."

"I'll be there even though John won't appreciate it," Thompson said. Then he finished his drink and left.

Duke looked at Bascomb, who was wiping up the ring of beer Bill Thompson's glass had left. He wondered if the sheriff had heard the gunshots. "It sounded like somebody did some shootin' a while ago."

"Oh?" Bascomb washed the glass and stared at Duke. "When was this? I didn't hear nothin'."

"Maybe I was mistaken," Duke said, finishing his beer. He set the glass on the bar and left.

Bill Thompson glanced through the bars of the cell and noticed that the figure he had constructed out of bedding and covered with a sheet was all askew. He unlocked the cell door and stepped inside. The sheet had six holes in it where the three shots had entered and exited.

"I'll be damned," he mumbled. "Colter was right." He silently cursed himself for not having asked Duke for his gun to check on whether or not it had been fired. On the other hand, he reasoned, there was no call to do that since he hadn't heard any shots. He thought briefly about returning to Bascomb's to arrest Duke, but decided against it because he would be unable to prove that Duke was the one who'd fired the shots into the dummy figure on the iron bunk. He cursed himself again for having left the jail unattended. Now he was just as helpless in bringing Alcott's murderer to justice as he was in bringing in Sarah Kittleman's killer.

If Colter was right in his reasoning, Duke was the man responsible for both deaths, but now there was no way to prove it. If he had been able to catch Duke redhanded in firing through the cell window, he might have sweated a confession to Sarah Kittleman's killing out of him as well as tag him for killing Alcott. As it was, he had nothing but suspicions.

Colter waited on a hill overlooking the main house on the Bar K spread until Kittleman and his crew of cowboys rode out toward town to attend Sarah's funeral. The only one remaining, as far as Colter could tell, was Carlos, the Mexican wrangler, and he was working out at the corrals. Colter rode as close to the house as he could without being seen. Then, leaving his horse in a small stand of trees, he circled the smokehouse and entered the main house through the rear door.

Making his way through the kitchen and the living room, he gazed at the broken window where the rifle bullet had entered. After checking the blood on the floor to determine where Sarah Kittleman had been sitting when she was shot, he followed the course of the bullet and spotted it lodged in the log wall opposite the window. He took a knife from his pocket and dug the bullet from the wall. It was a .52-caliber and came from the same Spencer that had killed Jack and had also fired at Colter when he had ridden over Jack's land looking for the vein of copper ore. He put it into his pocket along with the knife he had used. Then, after peering out of the window to make sure Carlos was still in the corral area, he turned and left the house.

Inside the jail, Walker Kriswell banged the broom into Thompson's boot as he attempted to sweep under the desk.

"Dammit, Walker, there's a foot inside that thing you know!" Thompson grumbled.

"I'm sorry, Sheriff. My eyes ain't as good as they was when I was your age."

A slight smile creased Thompson's face. "You ain't never been my age . . . Aw, hell, I shouldn't be bellowin' at you. It's that goddamned Kittleman that's got me wound up so tight."

"Didn't they bury his wife today over at the churchyard?"

"Yeah, they did. I've known Sarah Kittleman for nearly twenty-five years. She was a good, kindhearted woman. A hell of a lot better than that stiff-necked husband of hers."

"I thought you was on friendly terms with him."

Thompson scratched his head. "I was until a few days ago. As long as I looked the other way when those boys of his got too rowdy, ever'thing was okay. But let me enforce the law where he or his men were concerned . . . well, that's somethin' else. The least he could have done was to let me help lower the casket. . . . I'm gonna get a drink over at Bascomb's. Lock the door when you're through."

There were several men at the tables and half a dozen at the bar when Colter peered in the window of Bascomb's Saloon. Sheridan Mason saw Colter as he entered but said nothing to Thompson, preferring to let Colter take the initiative.

Colter nodded to Sheridan. " 'Evening."

Thompson recognized the voice and spun around, preparing to draw, but Colter's steady gaze stopped him. "What are you doing in here? I thought you'd be long gone by now."

"Now, Sheriff, you know that ain't true. I've been out to the Bar K lookin' around, and guess what I found?"

"You're damned lucky you didn't get yourself shot," Sheridan observed. "You're not exactly popular with Kittleman and his bunch."

Colter grinned as he took the three lead slugs from his pocket. "I know and I'm goin' to be even less popular when I show the sheriff here what I found." He dropped the three slugs on the bar as Bascomb came up.

"What'll you have, Colter?"

"Give him some of your private stock, Bascomb," Sheridan put in.

As Bascomb went back to get some of his good whiskey, Colter spoke to Thompson. "You saw the other two before . . . the one that killed Jack and the other one that just missed me when I rode out to Jack's ranch. The third one I dug out of Kittleman's dining-room wall this afternoon when everybody left."

Sheridan gazed at the three lead slugs. "They certainly look like triplets."

"They don't prove anything," Thompson said.

Colter stared in disbelief. "What in the hell do you need as proof?"

"I guess he expects you to bring Duke in with his finger still wrapped around the trigger of that Spencer," Sheridan said in mock seriousness.

"I don't expect him to do anything. He's not the law," Thompson grumbled.

"Well, it doesn't seem like you are either, Bill," Sheridan snapped.

"I'll tell you somethin', Sheriff. If you don't bring Duke in, I will, and it won't be to stand trial."

"Nobody tells me how to run my job, Colter. I'm through takin' orders."

"Is it Kittleman you're afraid of, or Duke?" Sheridan asked.

Thompson turned and glared at Sheridan. "If you weren't so damned old, I'd punch you right in the mouth. I said I'm through taking orders, and that includes insults as well." He glanced at Colter. "All right, I'll bring Duke in first thing in the morning. Right now I'm going to get drunk. By the way, that dummy I made up to look like Hank Alcott is full of holes. Unfortunately I didn't see who did it."

Sheridan's eyes narrowed. "Dummy? You mean you don't have Alcott in the jail?"

"Alcott's dead," Colter said. "Duke killed him."

"You *suspect* Duke killed him," the sheriff said.

"Suspect, hell! I know Duke killed him, and what's more, Thompson, so do you."

Sheridan shook his head. "I'm missing something here."

Colter explained about his suspicions of Duke and how he had predicted that Duke would try to kill Alcott for sure if he thought the man was still alive and able to identify him.

"The bullet-riddled dummy is proof enough, don't you think?" he asked.

Sheridan nodded. "It's enough for me. How about you, Bill?"

"I said I'd bring him in tomorrow, didn't I?" Thompson growled. He downed his drink and glared at both Sheridan and Colter. "I'll do my drinkin' some place else. Too damned much talk in here." With that he turned and walked out the door.

"What in the hell's eating him?" Sheridan asked.

"He's not as young or as fast as he was a few years

back, and he knows it. He's got to go up against Duke tomorrow. Duke's not that quick, but he's no slouch either, and he's got Kittleman behind him. I would offer to help him, but the man's developed some pride lately, and he'd just refuse it. Besides, if I were to ride out there with him, Kittleman might be forced to fight, and he'd get himself killed. As it is, I'm sure Kittleman figures that Duke can take care of himself without any help.''

"So you're not going to do anything?''

"Not until I see what happens tomorrow. If Thompson gets himself shot up, I'll bring Duke in myself.''

"What if Kittleman throws in with Duke?''

"I'll handle that problem when I come to it,'' Colter said, grinning. "Now, let's have another shot of Bascomb's Old Panther.''

After another half-hour of conversation with Sheridan, the subject of Amos and Johnny came up. Colter realized that he hadn't checked back to find out how Amos' wounded arm was getting along, and since he felt responsible for the old man getting shot, he thought it best to ride out and look in on him before hitting the hay for the night.

In answer to Colter's knock, Amos' voice boomed, "Who is it, and what in the hell do you want?''

"It's Colter Haines, Amos. I came out to see if you were still kickin'. I can tell you're all right by that warm friendly greeting.'' He could hear a laugh before the door opened.

"You liked that, did you?'' Amos asked, still chuckling as he opened the door.

"It's him, Pa!'' Johnny shouted, beaming.

"Yeah, it shore is. Come in.''

Colter stepped inside. "How's that arm? Did Doc Thatcher ever get out here to patch it up for you?''

"Yeah, but he's such a goddamned grouch, he takes

all the fun out of bein' waited on. I'll bet when he was a kid his ma had to tie pork chops around his neck to get the family dog to like him."

Colter laughed.

"What in tarnation are you a-doin' out here at this time of the night anyhow?"

"This time of the night? Hell, it's only eight o'clock."

"I've been in bed for an hour."

"Well, I don't want you to lose any beauty sleep, so I won't stay but a minute."

"Hell, I ain't never gonna git no purttier, so you might as well sit. Put the coffeepot on, Johnny."

"Yeah, coffee," Johnny said, running to the stove.

Colter told Amos what had happened since they had last seen each other, how he had dug the .52-caliber slug from the wall, how Duke had killed Alcott, how he and the sheriff had schemed to catch Duke in a trap, and how Duke had shot the dummy in the jail.

"I always knowed that lard-ass horse turd was no good, but I shore never figured he'd be so bad as to shoot Miz Kittleman. Why, she was a mother to that sidewinder for the last fifteen or twenty years."

"I know. That's why John Kittleman's goin' to find it so hard to believe when Thompson tells him about it tomorrow."

"Thompson will git hisself blowed to hell tomorrow. Just you wait and see. Kittleman ain't never gonna admit that he made a mistake in judgment when it comes to Duke."

"If Thompson can't bring him in, I'll do it myself."

"Then, by God, I'm goin' with you and don't tell me I can't. There ain't a damn thing you can do about it neither."

"Fine."

"I don't care what you say. I've got a claim to stake out on that bastard's hide, and I'm entitled to it."

"Good!"

"You think, just 'cause I'm old, that I ain't worth a tinker's dam. Well, I'll tell you that I . . . Huh?"

"I said fine—good! Come along. Glad to have you."

"Well, I'll be jiggered. You hear that, Johnny. I'm goin' with him to bring in Duke."

"Yeah, Duke. I'll git my horse."

"*You* ain't goin'. *I'm* goin'. Yore stayin' and there ain't no two ways about it. Now git that coffee up here before I fart in yore mess kit."

Johnny slunk back to the stove, muttering all the while.

The talk continued on into the night. Amos then convinced Colter that he should stay overnight since the Bar K Ranch was fairly close by and the road to town lay just a mile east of the cabin.

"We can ride down to a spot that overlooks the road that leads into Kittleman's place and wait for the sheriff. If he comes out with Duke, we'll ride along with him to town just in case the Bar K bunch gits some ideas about helpin' Duke git away. And if Thompson comes out feet-first, we'll know before anyone else in town does, and we can go after him."

"Sounds good," Colter said. "Let's sleep on it."

Shortly after eight o'clock the following morning, Colter and Amos sat on horseback watching the road that led to the Bar K Ranch.

"Instead of waiting for Thompson to ride in alone and get himself killed, I think we ought to go in with him," Colter said. "After all, I did shoot his deputy."

"I was thinkin' the same thing," Amos replied. "I don't like the bastard at all, but I'd shore hate to have the likes of Duke gun him down."

A lone rider caught their attention. It was Sheriff Thompson. They nudged their horses into a gentle lope on a course that would bring them to the road in time to meet Thompson.

Thompson looked up as the two riders came down the side of the hill. He recognized Colter immediately, and after a moment's hesitation, did the same with Amos. He continued riding and met them a hundred yards down the road.

Colter studied Thompson's face as he and Amos eased their mounts into a walk along side the lawman's horse. "We thought we'd give you a little company this mornin'," he said.

"I can do the job by myself. I don't need no help."

Amos started to comment, but Colter cut him off with a look and a slight shake of the head.

"We know that, Sheriff, but we're goin' along anyways just to make sure that Kittleman and his bunch don't try to stop you from doin' your sworn duty."

Thompson was glad that they had come along, but his newfound pride kept him from showing it. "It's a free country. You can ride wherever you want to."

They continued the rest of their journey in silence, broken only by an occasional muttering from Amos. As they rode through the entrance to the Bar K, Thompson dropped his right hand down by the side of his holster, Amos drew the double-barreled shotgun from its scabbard, and Colter eased the leather tie-down thong off the hammer of his Colt.

15

One of the Bar K wranglers, seeing the three men riding in, ran to the house to alert John Kittleman. He came out again followed by his boss, and the two of them stood for a moment looking at the riders. When Kittleman recognized them, he sent the wrangler running for a horse to ride out on the range and bring back Duke and some of the boys.

Thompson, Colter, and Amos rode into the front yard and stopped in a spread-out line facing Kittleman.

Kittleman spoke first. "What in the hell do you want?" He eyed Colter with hatred, then spoke again to Thompson. "You ridin' with murderers now?"

"No," Thompson replied slowly. "I came out here to bring one in."

"And who's that supposed to be?"

"Your foreman, Duke Stull."

"If you've got guts enough to tell him to his face, you can have that pleasure in a few minutes. I've already sent for him. Who is he supposed to have murdered?"

"My brother, for openers," Colter said.

"I don't believe I was talkin' to you, Haines."

"Well, he's talkin' to you, and you'd damn well better listen," Amos thundered.

"Your brother was killed by a man named Kramer," Kittleman snapped.

"My brother was killed by your foreman. He had a rifle slug through his back, and that ain't all."

"He also killed Hank Alcott," Thompson put in.

"The hell you say," Kittleman growled.

"Does Duke have a Spencer rifle, a fifty-two-caliber Spencer?" Colter asked.

"I don't know," Kittleman countered. "But what if he does? That doesn't prove anything."

"Let's see the rifle," Thompson said.

Kittleman yelled to one of his men, who was loitering near the bunkhouse watching what was going on, and told him to bring Duke's rifle if it was there. The man disappeared inside and reappeared a few moments later carrying the gun.

"Let me have it," Thompson ordered. He took the rifle and inspected it. "It's a Spencer, all right. Got a big bore too."

Duke and four riders came galloping into the yard from behind the bunkhouse area and reined to a halt near Kittleman but facing Colter and the others.

Kittleman glanced at Duke. "Thompson and Haines here were just telling me that you killed Jack Haines and Hank Alcott." He chuckled.

"What proof have they got?" Duke sneered.

"Enough," Thompson said. He took the three slugs Colter had given him from his shirt pocket. Holding them out toward Kittleman he said, "You may want to take a look at these, John. One of them was taken from Jack Haines' chest. It came in through the back. Another one came from a sandbank when someone tried to ambush Colter."

"What about the third one?" Duke asked. "Is that the one I'm supposed to have shot Alcott with?"

"No," Colter said. "You killed him with a handgun That third one," he said, glancing quickly at Kittleman and then back to Duke, "came from your dining-room wall, Mr. Kittleman. It buried into the wood after it killed your wife. They all came from the same rifle, the one Thompson's holding, Duke's fifty-two-caliber Spencer.''

''You're a liar!'' Duke shouted as he drew his gun. He was joined by three of the four men who had ridden in with him. There was an explosion of gunfire as the four Bar K riders fired at the same time that Thompson, Colter, and Amos opened up. Amos' shotgun blast blew one rider out of his saddle. Duke's bullet struck Thompson's frightened horse as it reared into the line of fire. Thompson fired, missing Duke but hitting one of the other two Bar K riders. Colter's bullet hit the fleshy upper part of Duke's left arm. One of the Bar K bullets caught Thompson in the shoulder. Another hit Amos in the arm, knocking him from the saddle. With the horses rearing, it was difficult to get in a clear shot. Colter fired again, hitting another Bar K rider. That left only Duke and one other man still mounted. They turned as Colter fired once more, missing both of them, and spurred their mounts into a run out of the yard.

Kittleman, who had stood open-mouthed during the brief flurry of gunfire, stepped over to look at Thompson, who lay sprawled on the ground.

Colter dismounted and helped Amos to his feet. ''You all right?''

''Yeah, I'll live. Don't let the son of a bitch git away. Go after him!''

''I'll find him. Don't worry about that. But first I want to get you to a doctor.''

''Thompson's hit bad,'' Kittleman observed. ''I'll get these men to town, and then I'll get some of the boys and we'll go after those two. I've been a fool.''

''I'll go now,'' Colter said. ''I don't like to follow a cold trail.''

''I'll send some men with you.''

Colter mounted. ''Haven't got time.'' He turned the

roan in the direction Duke and his friend had taken and galloped out of the yard.

Duke and McQueen pushed their horses until they reached the edge of the San Pedro River and then eased them back to a walk to let them breathe.

"Where are we runnin' to, Duke?" McQueen asked. "We headed for Tucson?"

"I got friends in Phoenix. That's where we're goin'. But first we got to shake Colter Haines off our trail. He'll probably figure on us ridin' north, but we ain't gonna do that. We're goin' west until we get about fifty miles beyond Santa Cruz River. Then we'll head north."

"You reckon he'll bring a posse with him?"

"No, he's a loner, but Kittleman sure as hell will. You can bet on that."

Colter kept the roan at a steady pace until he reached the San Pedro. Then, easing up to a walk, he guided the big horse into the river. When they reached the western bank, he dismounted and rolled himself a cigarette while he studied the tracks. There were numerous sets scattered about since the crossing he'd just made was on a well-traveled trail, but the ones he was seeking were not difficult to follow. He smiled as he picked out the set that had a slightly pigeon-toed left front hoof. The set that had accompanied Duke's pigeon-toed horse was smaller than average but had no distinctive features. Tracking Duke and McQueen would be no problem. Staying alive long enough to find them and bring them out was a mule of a different color. Colter didn't know anything about McQueen, but he knew for certain that Duke had no Indian-country knowledge. He was willing to bet that between the two of them, they couldn't drum up three days' experience riding the red man's trails. With a little luck, he thought grimly, they may not gain any experience on this trip either. He mounted the gelding once again and followed the two sets of tracks into Apache country.

He suspected that Duke and McQueen were headed for either Tucson or Phoenix, but had foolishly chosen to try to shake him from their trail by riding into Apache country. If they survived, they might be able to pull it off, for Colter himself stood a good chance of being caught or killed. The thought of dying the way Apaches put their prisoners to death was a bitter thing to contemplate. He gave considerable thought to turning back and riding to Tucson and Phoenix to wait and let Duke and McQueen take the chances, but after some soul-searching, he turned the idea down. He knew that they could turn south and head for Mexico, and if they did that, there would be no way of his knowing whether they had escaped or been captured and killed. That prospect disturbed him too much to give it more than a passing thought. No, he decided, there was only one thing to do: follow them and hope that he could bring them back alive to stand trial.

The tracks Colter was following continued due west, branching off from the other tracks that came down from the north. He followed the prints until they crossed a stretch of bare exposed rock and then lost them. He doubled back and dismounted at the spot where they were clearly visible for the last time. Then, leading the roan, he set off on foot, carefully checking the hard surface for signs of scuff marks that metal shoes would make if they struck just right. He soon found what he was looking for, a chip knocked from the ridge of rock that angled up the side of the arroyo he was in. He did not want to follow Duke's trail along the crest of the arroyo. Anyone foolish enough to silhouette himself against the sky in Indian country was asking to have his hair lifted.

Colter mounted and rode the bottom of the arroyo until it began to rise and the rim began to drop. They met a quarter of a mile farther on where the land flattened out. Noticing a wet spot in the sand ahead, he stopped and dismounted. The moist area was still warm where Duke's horse had relieved itself. That meant they were only minutes ahead. He climbed back into the saddle and nudged the roan into a fast walk. It was far less noisy than a gallop, and since it was only minutes till sunset, they might be setting up a campsite.

A long agonizing scream split the desert silence like a thunderclap. Colter reined to a halt. That kind of yell came only from the pain of torture. He listened intently and then heard the unmistakable sound of Apache language and laughter coming from beyond an outcrop of granite that loomed ahead on his left. Guiding his horse to the back side of the rocks, Colter dismounted and kept his hand on the gelding's muzzle. When the horse seemed to have settled down, he left it and cautiously moved to a break in the rock formation.

Colter studied the small band of Apaches that stood watching two of their fellow warriors at work on the prisoners. When it comes to torture, the Apaches have few peers. They are masters at it, and they enjoy it, and this band, Colter knew, was enjoying it immensely.

Duke and McQueen were staked spread-eagled on the ground near a small fire. They were naked from the waist up. Their tormentors each had a mesquite branch with a couple of inches of hot glowing embers at the ends. These were pressed into the tender armpits of the two cowboys, who screamed in agony.

As much as Colter hated Duke for killing Jack, he hated to see anyone tortured even more. He felt that no one deserved that kind of death, for surely they would die, and what they were going through now was just the beginning.

Fortunately for Duke and McQueen, the sun was setting and it would soon be dark. Apaches, like most men who enjoy torturing others, want to be able to get the greatest pleasure from their acts, and most of that is visual. When darkness comes—and especially when one is trying to evade capture by the U.S. Army—one does not keep fires burning. Colter knew that the Indians would be putting the fire out. Until then, Duke and his friend would have to endure whatever came their way, for Colter would not, could not make a move to help them against their attackers until it was dark without putting his own life in jeopardy.

He waited, as patiently as a man can in the presence of tortured screams, and studied the situation. There were eight Apaches. Their horses—six of them tough, unshod mustangs, two of them bigger, shod, and branded Army mounts—and the two horses of Duke and McQueen were tethered in a small ravine about twenty yards beyond. The Apaches would undoubtedly post a guard for the night and the logical spot would be the high point nearest the camp, the rocks where Colter now waited. A plan began to formulate in his mind. He smiled grimly. It may work. It had to work, or Duke and McQueen would soon be mutilated corpses, come sunrise.

Darkness came with the sudden swiftness typical of the desert. Dusk, if it was there at all, was a fleeting moment of half-light. Colter huddled out of sight behind a creosote bush and waited. The slender crescent of a new moon provided a small bit of light to an otherwise dark desert floor.

After the Apaches had been asleep for an hour, Colter began working his way toward the lone brave standing guard. He had removed his boots and slipped on the moccasins that he always carried for such emer-

gencies. When he had reached a spot some five yards
from the guard, he stopped. The ground sloped downward for a few feet, then took a more rapid descent
until it reached the desert floor, where it leveled out.
Colter took a round rock and rolled it down a small
weed-strewn crevice that angled toward the camp the
warriors had made at the base of the rock cluster.

The stone, moving through the dry vegetation, made
a rustling sound such as a snake or bird might do. The
Apache guard turned in the direction of the noise and
raised himself cautiously to a standing position to investigate. Colter, moving on moccasined feet, covered
the distance between himself and the brave in an instant. Bringing his Colt down in a crushing blow, he
caught the guard just behind the right ear and dropped
him in a soundless heap on the hard surface of the
rocky outcrop. Then, moving cautiously, he skirted
the camp and crawled into the ravine where the horses
stood in mute silence. He gathered dry tumbleweeds
and brush and bound them together with a buckskin
thong. Leaving the brush for a moment, he skirted the
outcrop of rock and checked the unconscious guard.
He was still out and would be for some time.

Colter took the reins of his roan and led him around
the rocks to a point slightly above the camp. He left
the gelding alone and walked back to the ravine. Taking a knife from his pocket, he cut the picket line and
led the ponies down the ravine away from the camp.
Then, untying Duke and McQueen's horses from the
rest, he took them back to join his roan.

He stopped and studied the sleeping Apaches. Lo-
cating the two white men, he moved down the ravine
again and emerged at a point a couple of yards from
the cowboys. Slipping his knife under the thongs that
held them to the stakes, he cut them. Then, placing a
hand over Duke's mouth, he gave him a shake. Duke
awoke with a start, his eyes wide with fear. Seeing

Colter, his expression changed to one of astonishment. Colter placed a finger against his lips, then gave McQueen a shake.

He got the two men to their feet and led them back to the ravine. When they reached the area where the mustangs were, he cut the animals loose and tied the bundle of dry brush to one end of the picket line and tied the other end to a mustang's hackamore. Turning the animal in the direction of the sleeping Indians, he took a match from his pocket.

"Mount up," he whispered.

Duke and McQueen pulled themselves onto their saddles.

"When we scatter their horses, those Apaches will wake up. I'm sending this one down there with a fire behind it. When I do, head east back toward the river," he said quietly. "All hell will break loose, so ride hard."

He lit the match and touched it to the dry brush. It exploded into flame. He mounted the roan, then leaned over and slapped the pony a hard blow on its rump. The terrified mustang, the fire burning at its hooves, burst through the Indian camp at a gallop. The other horses scattered in different directions.

The Apaches were on their feet the moment the mustang hit their camp. They expected an army patrol, but when none materialized, they realized that a rescue effort was under way and consequently tried to catch any of the horses that came within reach.

One of the warriors grabbed a horse as it ran by and hung on to its neck until it finally stopped. Then, swinging himself up on its back, he turned in the direction the three riders had taken and savagely kicked it into a dead run.

Colter's first indication that they were being followed was when a rifle shot cracked close by and tore through a tree branch near his head. He glanced over his shoulder and saw the Apache gaining ground. He drew his Colt from its holster, but before he could turn and shoot, the Apache fired again, and the slug slammed into Colter's back. The blow knocked him forward so that he fell over the saddle horn but stayed mounted. He twisted his body slightly and fired. The .45 bullet hit the Apache in the chest. He dropped his rifle and tried desperately to hang on to the hackamore, but the lead had split when it struck a rib and had torn through the warrior's lung, leaving two distinct holes as it exited. He lost his grip on the leather hackamore and fell heavily to the ground.

The Apache bullet had plowed into Colter's back along his left side about even with his elbow, forcing its way between two ribs, then altered its direction slightly and took a portion of a third rib with it as it tore an exit through the lower part of his chest about two inches below the pectoral muscle. It was not a dangerous wound in that it struck neither a vital organ nor an artery, but it was painful and Colter knew that any wound caused by lead had great infection potential if left untreated for a while. And, he was still miles and hours away from medical attention.

He decided that it would be best if he could keep his wound a secret from Duke and McQueen. Neither of them was armed, and they were both without shirts, but they would be freezing in the cold night air of the desert, and after their torture by the Apaches, they would certainly be in an ugly mood.

After they had ridden for about a half-hour, Colter called for them to ease up to a walk. "They won't be catching us now," he said.

"I ain't too sure about that," McQueen replied. "I want as much distance between me and them devils as I can get." He started to spur his horse into a gallop again.

"Hold it!" Colter barked. "Either that horse walks right now, or you do."

"We're freezin' our butts off, Haines," Duke complained. "You aimin' to keep us walkin' these animals all night?"

"Hell, at this rate we'll die from the cold before them Apaches kill us," McQueen put in.

"That wouldn't be any great loss," Colter said.

As they rode along in silence, broken only by the occasional grumble of the two men and the clicking of the horses' shoes against hidden rocks, Colter thought about McQueen's voice. It had a Scottish accent, not a thick burr, but it was there nevertheless. It suddenly dawned on him that this was the voice Cynthia Dobbs had heard that night in town when someone—someone with a funny accent—had tried to ambush him. McQueen was the hombre who had talked with Hank Alcott that night in the alley behind Alcott's store. Colter smiled grimly. He had been right about Alcott all along.

He took a bandanna from his pocket and pressed it against the hole the bullet had ripped on its exit through his ribs. Blood had drained down his side and collected at his belt, soaking both his shirt and his pants around the waist and left hip area.

He faced a dilemma that presented several unwelcome alternatives. If they kept the horses at a walk, his wound was less likely to bleed as much, but it also allowed the Apaches, if they chose, time to catch up, assuming that they had managed to round up their mustangs. On the other hand, if they urged their own mounts into a slow gallop, the constant rocking motion would aggravate the wound and it would bleed even more. He would then lose consciousness and both Duke and McQueen would be on him in an instant. Also running a horse in the dark over unknown ground should be done only as a last resort, in Colter's opinion. It was just asking for the animal to step into a prairie-dog hole or fall into one of the many small ravines cut into the desert's rough face by innumerable flash floods, and then break a leg or kill the rider. He opted for continuing to move at a fast walk.

Duke and McQueen rode ahead of Colter, shivering from the cold and muttering to themselves.

"I ca-can't stand this co-cold much longer," McQueen complained. "I think we ought to ju-jump him."

"He'd shoot us down in a second," Duke answered. "But I think if we hold off a little longer, we'll be able to ride off without any problems."

"What you talkin' about?"

"I'm talkin' about him bein' hit. One of them 'Pache bullets must have winged him. I've been watchin' and he's near fell out of the saddle two or three times."

McQueen glanced back over his shoulder and noticed Colter weaving around in the saddle. "I think you're right," he said excitedly. "He damned near fe-fell just then."

As the horses entered an arroyo, Duke guided his close to one of the banks and grabbed a rock from its dry surface. He showed his prize to McQueen and smiled. When Colter's roan started down the embankment toward the bottom of the arroyo, Duke turned and threw the rock. It hit Colter in the upper part of his chest, knocking him backward. As he fell, he pulled the reins back so sharply that the roan reared up on his hind legs. That action, coupled with his weakened condition, forced Colter to fall off the horse. He landed unconscious on the arroyo floor.

Duke turned and jumped off his horse. He yanked Colter's gun from its holster and was about to finish him off when McQueen spoke.

"Don't shoot, Duke! If them Apaches are around, they'll hear it. He ain't gonna live long if we take his coat, his shirt, his water, and his horse. If the wound or the cold don't kill him, them Indians will.''

Duke let the hammer back down and stuck the gun in his belt. "You get his horse, and I'll strip off his coat and his shirt.''

McQueen rode up to the side of Colter's roan and reached for its reins. The big gelding shied away. McQueen tried again, speaking to the horse in soothing tones. The roan refused to let the man take his bridle.

"Stand still, damn you!" McQueen cursed. The roan trotted off with McQueen in pursuit. When he had been gone for ten minutes, he returned without the roan.

"That damned horse must be part mountain goat. Couldn't get near the son of a bitch. At least I ran him off so Colter can't get him when he wakes up.''

Duke handed McQueen Colter's bloodsoaked shirt. "Here, better put it on.''

"How come I don't get to wear his coat? I'm a hell of a lot colder than you are.''

"Matter of opinion," Duke said, mounting up. "Let's ride.'' He touched a spur to his horse's flank, and it took off.

"I ain't as fat as you are," McQueen said quietly. "If I was, I wouldn't mind the cold either.''

"What'd you say?" Duke growled.

"Nothin'," McQueen mumbled.

Colter awoke cold, stiff, and dizzy. He was weak from the loss of blood. His wound had reopened as a result of his fall and his side ached something awful. Sitting up, he looked around and finally got his bearings. He had a new ache, just below the clavicle where Duke's rock had struck. Worst of all, his pride had taken a beating. He was angry at himself for letting Duke get the jump on him. He knew he should have been more alert, but his wound had dulled his thinking, made his reactions slower. He cursed himself for having ridden into Apache country in the first place. He should have ridden out once he saw the warriors applying the hot brands to Duke's and McQueen's bodies. That way they would have both gotten their retribution at no risk to himself. He stood on rubbery legs and searched the darkness for his horse. He knew the roan wouldn't tolerate a stranger handling his reins if it were at all possible. Puckering his lips, he let out a long, high whistle and then listened. Within a few minutes he heard the hooves thud in the sand and then stop, uncertain of the direction. He whistled again and the roan came up and whinnied softly, giving his arm a nudge.

Colter grinned. "I'm sure glad to see you, fella." He untied the slicker and a blanket. Wrapping the blanket around his shoulders and waist, he slipped the raincoat on over the top of the blanket and buttoned it up. Then, with his last ounce of strength, he pulled himself into the saddle and headed for the San Pedro.

He didn't realize he had been asleep until he woke up and found himself draped over the roan's neck staring straight down into the water of the San Pedro. With effort he sat upright and looked around. It was getting light in the east and the opposite bank was clearly defined. He nudged the gelding across the main part of the river and then up the other side. When he reached dry land, he stopped and thought for a bit. He needed rest badly, but there was a problem with stopping. If the wound continued to bleed while he slept, he just might never wake up, and even if he did, he might not have the strength to get into the saddle again. He decided to continue on riding. Amos' house couldn't be more than ten miles away. If he could just hold out until then . . .

Amos Carson stood scratching his rear through the torn flap of his long johns. He ran a gnarled hand

through his thick thatch of gray hair and then yelled
at his son.

"Johnny, it's time to rise and shine. God's made us
another beautiful day. Let's git out and take a look at
it. You fetch the coffee water and I'll git this fire a-
goin'." The stitches in his wound pulled as he bent
over, causing him to grumble.

Johnny sprang out of bed, grabbed the big blackened
coffeepot from the back burner of the stove, and ran
outside, barefoot and in his long johns. He was back
in a few seconds full of excitement. "He's here, Pa.
It's him."

"Who's here? Who's him?"

Johnny pointed excitedly out the open door. "He's
there just a-sittin'. It's him."

Amos took his rifle from its peg on the wall and
stepped outside. "Who are you talkin' about, boy?"

Johnny pointed at Colter, who lay facedown over
the neck of his horse. The roan stood near the sheep
pen on the hill behind the cabin, stamping impatiently.

"We'll I'll be a suck-egg mule if that don't look
like Colter. He's done got hisself all shot up again,
from the looks of it. Go bring his horse down here,
Johnny, and let's carry him into the house."

Johnny, still barefoot and in his underwear, took off
at a run. He was back in a few moments leading the
roan with Colter about ready to slide off. He and Amos
carried Colter into the house and put him on a bed.
Amos removed the slicker and blanket from Colter's
unconscious body and gave a quick examination of his
wounds.

"He's been backshot," he announced. "Most likely
it was that fat-assed Duke or that snake of a pardner
of his."

"Yeah, a snake!" Johnny said.

"Well, it don't look too dangerous," Amos commented, "but he's lost a couple of gallons of blood, from the looks of things. Git a fire goin' and stick that bowie knife in it so we can heat the blade. We need to sear the meat around this hole here to keep him from losin' any more blood. Don't stick the whole knife in the fire, you knothead, just the blade."

Johnny reached into the fire and extracted the big knife. Then, sticking just the blade back into the crackling flames, he announced, "Yeah, the blade."

Amos cauterized the wound and bound it with a bandage made from a strip of torn sheet. He then pulled a pot of lamb stew from the back burner to the front and heated it for Colter's breakfast.

Colter slept for another three hours before he woke up. When he finally did open his eyes, Amos was sitting in a chair next to the bed staring at him.

"Seems like I'm always imposing on your hospitality, Amos. How's that arm of yours? Are you able to use it okay?"

Amos grinned. "If I could just drop it around Duke's neck, I'd show you how good it is. How'd you git all shot up?"

Colter explained what had happened in the last twenty-four hours, how Duke had knocked him from the saddle with a rock and how they'd left him for dead in Apache territory.

"That's exactly what I'd expect from that potbellied, slop-eatin', egg-suckin' bastard. You save his hide from them 'Paches and look what you git in return. They steal the shirt off yore back and leave you to die among the heathens."

"They're desperate men, Amos. They're gonna do everything they can to stay alive."

"I'd shore like to draw a bead on them buggers. Neither one of 'em's worth a pound of sour owl manure. You should have left 'em for the Injuns to take care of. Here, you'd better start eatin' somethin' or you ain't gonna git strong enough to go after them two scorpions.''

Colter sat up and began eating some of the lamb stew Amos set before him. Johnny squatted on his haunches and stared intently at Colter while he ate. Colter paused in his eating for a moment and winked at Johnny and then gave him a big grin. "How are you doin', Johnny?''

Johnny grinned. "Fine. Yeah!''

Amos smiled. He liked Colter's interest in Johnny. Very few people took the time to talk to the boy at all, except for a few like Duke, who enjoyed ridiculing him.

"I should be ready to ride by tonight,'' Colter said. "I've got to catch them before they get too far away. I see you're doin' all right. How's Thompson?''

"He was hit purty hard, and you ain't doin' too well neither. You got a hole in yore side you can stick a cord of wood in. You ain't ridin' tonight, nor tomorrow neither. Yore stayin' in that bed till you git yore strength back, and I don't give a hoot and a holler if it takes a week.''

Colter grinned and winked at Johnny again. "He sounds kinda mean, doesn't he?''

Johnny laughed and slapped his knee. "Yeah! Mean! Yeah!''

16

Colter took Amos' advice and rested for a week. He felt positive that Duke and McQueen would head for either Tucson or Phoenix. Amos had brought word from town that Duke had friends north of Charleston, friends who would protect him if he needed it.

At the end of the week that Colter had spent recuperating, the wound in his back had scabbed over enough to be well on its way to healing completely. Where the bullet had made its exit, however, had not healed enough, enough to suit Amos. Colter felt ready to ride even though there was still considerable soreness. Cynthia Dobbs, who had come out at Amos' invitation, felt the same way as her host. She told Colter that he should let the law take care of finding Duke and McQueen. He was almost convinced that she was right when John Kittleman rode up, accompanied by eight of his men.

Amos was instantly suspicious. "Now what in the hell does he want? He's got a nerve ridin' onto my property."

"Well, let's ask him," Colter commented, stepping into the yard in front of the cabin.

"Haines, I've come to do two things. First, I want to say I've been wrong about you, and I've sure been wrong about Duke. I'm here to say I'm sorry for the way you've been treated by me and my men. The same goes for you and your son, Mr. Carson. You'll have no more trouble from the Bar K from now on. The second thing is, I've got word that Duke and McQueen are holed up at the Flying W Ranch just this side of Phoenix. We're riding now and you're welcome to join us if you'd like. You too, Mr. Carson, if you care to come.''

"I'll saddle my horse," Colter said.

"I'm goin' with you," Amos added.

Colter put his hand on Amos' shoulder. "I appreciate your wanting to go along, but you took a slug yourself just a few days ago, and it's not healed yet. Besides, what would happen to Johnny if you got yourself killed?"

"He's right, Mr. Carson," Cynthia said. "It's bad enough for him to be riding with his side still not healed properly without you doing the same thing."

Colter was back in a couple of minutes, sitting astride his roan. "We shouldn't be gone more than a few days," he said, looking at Cynthia.

"Few days, hell!" Amos grumbled. "It's two hundred miles to Phoenix. You'll be a week at least."

"That ain't too long," Colter answered, grinning. "Take care of him, Cynthia, and don't let his growling scare you. He's really harmless."

"Yeah!" Johnny said, slapping his leg and laughing. "Yeah . . . harmless!"

As Colter turned to ride, Cynthia spoke. "Colter, be careful, please."

Colter's face softened as he gazed at her beauty. "I'll be back." He drew the reins across the roan's neck and it turned in the direction that Kittleman and his hands had taken.

The ride north was hard for Colter. His wound occasionally seeped a little blood, and it was continually painful. Kittleman was determined that they should catch Duke and McQueen as soon as possible, so there was no letup on the constant push to Phoenix.

Two days later, after they had learned that Duke and McQueen were not at the Flying W Ranch, they sighted the outskirts of town.

Kittleman raised his hand in a signal to stop, then spoke to Colter. "I feel that we should split up and come into town from both ends at the same time. That way, if someone does happen to see us and warns that no-good son of a bitch, we'll be able to stop him from getting away. What do you think?"

"It sounds okay to me as long as whoever finds him first waits until the others have come up and taken positions."

"Fair enough. Why don't you and half of these boys stay on this end of the street, and I'll take the other half with me and we'll ride to the far end."

Colter waited until he could see Kittleman working his way toward him from the far end of the street. Then he and the others rode along, stopping and checking at each saloon. Then he spotted the Bar K brand on two horses outside a bar and sent one of the riders up the street to bring Kittleman back.

"Do we call 'em out or go in and get 'em?" someone asked.

"We go in," Colter said. "Otherwise we can have people shooting at us from the windows."

They dismounted and walked into the saloon.

Duke was standing at the bar with his back to the door. There were at least a dozen men having a drink. McQueen, who was leaning on one elbow laughing at a joke, saw them first.

"Duke!" he yelled.

Duke turned, as did Frank Wallen, owner of the Flying W. The cowboys who were not part of the Flying W crew cleared a spot on either side of the Flying W bunch. It was not difficult for them to spot trouble coming.

Kittleman spoke, looking straight at Frank Wallen.

"We've come here to take a murderer back to Charleston. We have no argument against any of you Flying W people. If you choose to make this your business, a lot of you will get hurt and some of you will die."

"Any of you people lawmen?" Frank Wallen asked.

"We didn't have time to find one," Kittleman replied, "but that's not important. This man has killed four people in our town. One of them was my wife and another one was this man's brother."

Wallen glared at Duke. "You didn't say nothin' about killin' no woman."

"I didn't" Duke lied. "They're tryin' to blame me for somethin' I didn't do."

"You're a liar, Duke," Colter said, "and you're a fool, mister, if you believe him."

"If he killed all those people, then why ain't the law with you?" Wallen asked.

"He would have been, but Duke shot him too," Kittleman said.

"Sounds like you're a regular one-man army," Wallen said, chuckling.

"Stand aside, fella. I'm takin' Duke and McQueen with me," Colter said.

As he started to move forward, McQueen stepped to one side. His lower lip began to quiver. "Wait a minute, Haines. I'm comin' with you peacefully. I ain't never killed nobody, and I don't aim to start in now. I took a couple of shots at you one night, but I never killed nobody."

As McQueen stepped forward, Duke drew his gun.

"You're a yella dog, McQueen." He shot McQueen in the back and then turned the gun toward Colter.

At the sound of Duke's gunshot, everyone dived for cover. Someone bumped into Colter and knocked him off balance. Duke's next bullet, meant for Colter, smashed into the chest of one of Kittleman's crew. Several shots were fired in the exchange. A moment later the sheriff entered and fired three shots into the ceiling.

"Hold it!" The gunshots ceased. "What in thunder's going on in here?"

Kittleman moved to the side of his wounded cowhand while Colter spoke.

"We came to take Duke Stull back to Charleston for murder when this fella and his boys decided we were wrong."

"Any of you totin' a badge?"

"No."

"Then you are wrong. Is this a legally constituted posse?"

"Legal enough, sheriff," Kittleman said. "Duke killed my wife, Colter's brother, and two others. He also shot and wounded the sheriff. I own the largest spread in Charleston, and you can take my word that my men and I are acting as legally as we can, under the circumstances."

"Frank, who was responsible for killing this man?"

"Duke, the man we were trying to take," Colter said.

"I asked Frank," the sheriff growled.

"He's right, Elmer. It was Duke. Shot him right in the back."

"Where is this Duke?" Elmer asked.

"I seen him skip out the back," someone said.

Colter started for the door.

"Where you going, cowboy?" Elmer asked.

"I'm goin' after Duke."

"Not unless you're part of a posse, you're not."

Colter glared at Elmer. "Sheriff, that man killed my brother and now he's got a head start. I'm not waitin' for you or anybody else. If you're goin' to stop me, do it now or you'll have to shoot me in the back."

The sheriff shifted uncomfortably. He knew from

the look on Colter's face that he would never back down.

Colter turned and went out the door.

"I'll deputize you later," the sheriff yelled.

Colter stepped into the saddle and looked at the hoof prints on the street. The ones made by a horse in a hurry headed south toward Mexico. He backed the gelding away from the rail and spurred it into a gallop toward the border.

Duke's horse with the toed-in front hoof was easy to follow. The hard riding to follow the prints, however, had caused Colter's wound to reopen and brought with it a lot of additional pain. Consequently he had to slow down, allowing Duke to increase the distance between them.

The first night Colter rode until nearly midnight and then stopped without having seen anything more than tracks. Once on the following day, as he was descending the side of a small hill, he caught sight of Duke as he traversed the last of a flat stretch of terrain. He was well over a mile away. It made the pain a little easier to bear knowing that he was so close to his quarry.

On the third day the sky darkened and the sliver of moon, such as it was, was no longer visible. He had to make camp early because of the darkness. He awakened with a light rain pelting him in the face. The gnawing pangs of hunger began to affect him. There was comfort in the fact that Duke, too, must be feeling the same thing. The nearest town where supplies could be had was Tucson, but Colter knew that Duke would steer clear of that town. There was a rancher who lived at Arrowhead Wells about thirty miles east of Tucson. Duke would most likely cut through the Santa Rosa Mountains and head for that ranch, if he knew it existed. The chances were that he didn't, but Colter had to plan on his knowing and take the proper action.

Besides, he needed food and water for himself and his mount, and the ranch was the only solution.

The following day Colter came to the ranch. He dismounted a hundred yards away and out of sight of the building itself. Then, working his way around a saguaro, he came to the back door of the ranch house. Drawing his gun, he carefully opened the door and stepped in. A gaunt-looking woman stood talking to a man who lay flat on his back on a bed. When Colter saw that Duke was not present, he backed out of the door and quietly closed it. Then, walking around to the front door, he knocked.

The gaunt woman called out. "Who is it, and what do you want?"

"My name's Colter Haines, ma'am. The fella I've been chasin' has been through here. If you need any help with your man's wounds, I'll be glad to help you."

The door opened a crack and a rifle barrel protruded through it. "How do you know about my man?"

"I came in the back door. If I was aimin' to rob you or shoot you, I could have done it then. I need some food and water if I'm to catch him."

The door opened all the way, and the woman stepped aside. "Mister, you're welcome to anything we've got if you're after that no-account lizard. He shot Walter for no reason at all. I said he could have food and water, but he needed money too, so he just gunned Walter down and robbed him."

"That's Duke, all right," Colter said. "He'd steal pennies from a dead man's eyes. If it's all right with you, ma'am, I'd be obliged if you let me stay here tonight. I don't want to lose his trail and it's startin' to get dark."

"Why, sure you're welcome to stay, young man. I'd be obliged to you if you'd help me put a splint on

Walter's arm. By the way, I'm Maggie Blevin.'' She extended her hand.

"Colter Haines,'' Colter said, giving her hand a shake. "I'll take care of the splint for you.''

"You do that, and I'll put some supper together.''

Colter took two flat pieces of wood from the wood box and some torn cloth that Maggie had already prepared and began tying a splint to Walter's arm where she had bandaged it.

Maggie talked as she cooked the meal. "Have you got any idea where that snake will go?''

"I'm betting on Sasabe. That's a little town just below the border. He may try Magdalena. That's a little bit bigger. Wherever he goes, I'm gonna be right on his tail.''

On the following morning after he had eaten breakfast and fed and watered his roan, he looked in on Walter Blevin and checked his splint and bandage.

Walter watched silently as Colter readjusted the bandage. When Colter finished and straightened up, Walter spoke.

"Mr. Haines, I'm much obliged for what you've done. If I felt up to it, I'd ride along with you in the hopes I'd get a shot at that fella Duke. He's about the meanest hombre I reckon I ever did see.''

"Mr. Blevin, if he gives me the slightest excuse, I'll pump at least two shots into him, one for me and one for you. How does that sound?''

Walter grinned. "You're my kind of man, Mr. Haines. Good luck.'' He reached out his hand and Colter shook it.

After Colter had gone, Maggie spoke to her husband. "Looks like Mr. Haines is packin' a reminder from that snake Duke.''

"What do you mean?''

"I saw him this morning washin' up with his shirt

off. He's got a bullet hole in his back and a big bandage over the place in front where it came out.''

"Yeah, that sounds like somethin' that Duke fella would do. I hope Haines blows him to kingdom come.''

"Maybe he might do that. The Lord's will works in mysterious ways,'' she said.

Colter felt more rested than he had in days. Maggie's cooking and a straw pallet to sleep on last night was what did it, he guessed. Even though there had been a light rain during the night, the tracks of Duke's horse were plainly visible. Colter found the remains of Duke's fire from the night before. From the looks of it, Duke was getting bolder. There had been only a halfhearted attempt to scatter the ashes and the remains of burnt twigs. Duke had dragged a boot through the remnants several times and then abandoned the idea.

Colter smiled. That's good, he thought. Old Duke is gettin' careless. I hope he keeps it up.

Early the following evening he could make out the outline of the collection of adobe buildings that made up Sasabe. By the time he reached the outskirts, it was dark and lamps were being lighted. He stopped outside the cantina and entered cautiously. Duke was nowhere in sight. He stepped to the bar.

"Una cerveza, por favor."

The bartender brought the beer and set it on the scarred wood surface that served as a bar. *"Cincuenta centavos."*

Colter drew five silver pesos from his pocket, put one on the bar, and held the other four. *"¿Habla Usted inglés, señor?"*

The bartender shrugged. *"Un poco."*

Colter described Duke to the bartender. "Have you seen him?"

"Tal vez."

"En inglés!"

"Perhaps, señor. But my—how you say, memory—she is not so good."

Colter dropped a peso on the bar. The bartender shrugged. He dropped another peso. The bartender smiled. "It is beginning to come back to me."

Colter dropped the other two pesos.

The bartender smiled. *"Sí.* Now I remember. He rode in this afternoon, drank some *cervezas,* talked to some vaqueros, and left."

"Did he say where he might be goin'?"

"My memory—she is not too good."

Colter fished another two pesos out of his pocket. "If this doesn't clear it up, I'm gonna have to try somethin' else."

The bartender didn't like the tone that had suddenly appeared in Colter's voice. It had an ominous sound to it.

"I think maybe she is clearing up again."

"Where was he headin' when he left here?"

"He said he was going to Nogales."

"Thanks."

"But he took the road to Magdalena."

Colter drew another peso from his pocket and dropped it on the bar.

"Have a *cerveza* on me."

"Gracias."

"Where is a good place to spend the night?"

"I have some *alcobas* in the back. Two pesos without and five pesos with."

"With what?"

"A lovely señorita."

"Like those two?" Colter nodded toward two buxom overweight women who stood drinking at the far end of the bar.

"Sí."

"Here's two pesos. Which room do I get?"

"The one *a la izquierda*. I mean. . ."

"I know . . . on the left."

"*Sí*. You know my language?"

"*Un poco*," Colter said. "I need food. I'm hungry."

"Ah, María Escobar serves the best tamales in Mexico. Go down to the end of this street. She is *a la* . . . she is on the left."

"*Gracias*, my friend."

Colter walked to the end of the street and found a small café on the left side. The bartender was right. María did serve the best tamales.

After he had eaten and found a place to leave his horse, he went back to the cantina and looked for the room he had paid for. He found it without too much difficulty. Once inside, he propped a chair under the doorknob, and then, after sticking his Colt under his pillow, he fell into a deep sleep.

A scraping sound brought Colter's eyes open with a snap. The chair he had propped under the doorknob was slowly being pushed inward as the door was forced open. Moonlight filtering through the shabby curtains at the window showed two men entering the room. Colter caught the gleam of light reflecting off the blade of a knife as the man nearest him raised it overhead. He swung the Colt from beneath his pillow and fired two quick shots. The man with the knife caught the first bullet in his chest and fell back against the spindle legs of a small table, and the resounding crash brought excited voices from outside. Colter's second bullet hit the other intruder in the shoulder, slamming him against the wall just as he squeezed off a shot of his own. The slug plowed into the saguaro-ribbed ceiling.

Colter leapt out of bed with his gun ready. He struck a match and looked at the two would-be killers. The knife man lay dead and the gunman wounded but alive.

Colter lit the small lamp that sat on top of a washstand. Then, turning his attention to the wounded gunman, he propped the man up in a sitting position.

"Why did you try to kill me?"

"No sé inglés."

Colter cocked the hammer back on his Colt and shoved it under the wounded man's nose. "Maybe this will help. It usually does."

"The other gringo who came through this afternoon, he said that you had robbed a *banco* and carried much money with you. I think he did not tell the truth."

"I think you are right," Colter said.

The bartender-owner came into the room wearing a nightshirt and carrying a shotgun.

"¿Qué pasó, amigo?"

"These vaquero friends of yours tried to kill me."

"They are not friends of mine, señor, only . . . how you say . . . acquaintances. They are the ones who talked to the gringo you seek." He looked at the dead knifer. "What a pity to get a big hole in a shirt of such quality." He stepped outside. "Jorge, Esteban, *vengan acá rápido.*" Stepping back inside he said, "My two sons will take this poor fool to the cemetery. The other one can walk. Get up and get out of here." He gave the wounded gunman a nudge with his boot. "We have no law here. You want me to kill him?"

Colter looked at the wounded man, who was obviously in pain. "No, just get him out of here so I can get some sleep."

The bartender's sons came into the room and removed the dead man. The wounded gunman staggered to his feet and went out with them.

Colter was once again left alone, but he was keyed up, restless, and unable to sleep. He checked his watch. It was almost three-thirty A.M. He rose and pulled on his boots. Then, after checking the outside, he stepped out and headed for the corral where he had left his horse.

Once astride the roan, he headed south toward Magdalena. By late afternoon he had reached the outskirts of the town. He rode down several of the dusty treeless streets without seeing Duke's horse at all. Finally, in the gathering darkness, he stopped at a cantina that had a delicious aroma of food wafting through a rear window. Once inside he ordered a plate of *frijoles* and *tortillas* and a *cerveza*. While he was eating, he studied the other people in the cantina.

Two old men sat discussing the land reforms of Benito Juárez. Three younger men sat at a table telling dirty stories. Two other men stood at the bar with a couple of overblown bar maids laughing at something that had happened the night before. No one seemed particularly interested in Colter's presence, which was very much to his liking.

After he had eaten and had a couple more beers, he went back outside. The soft strumming of a guitar brought thoughts of Cynthia Dobbs flickering across Colter's mind. He missed her. For the first time the possibility of his dying here in Mexico hit him. He didn't like the thought of being backshot in some dark street by Duke Stull. If Duke killed him, no one would know where he was. The idea of lying in an unmarked grave in a foreign country appalled him. The way to remedy the situation, of course, was to find Duke and take him back . . . or kill him. He couldn't afford to give Duke the first shot.

Keeping in the shadow, he went along the street peering into any place that had a lamp burning. After having gone from one end of town to the other without success, he returned to the cantina hitching rail and got his horse. Mounting up, he rode out of town and made a dry camp for the night. The attempt on his life the previous evening made him edgy and he didn't want another situation like that one to happen again.

The following morning he rose and stretched, thinking how good it was to be alive. After having some jerky and hardtack that Maggie Blevin had given him, he saddled the roan and headed back to town. He decided to have coffee at the cantina and play the waiting game.

Just before twelve noon, the cantina began to fill up. It was a larger crowd than the one from the previous evening. Many were Mexican vaqueros with an occasional farmer in his traditional white clothing and sandals seeming out of place and somewhat uncomfortable as he drank his *cerveza*. Most of the vaqueros preferred tequila and a slice of lime to the *cerveza*, which was really too warm for Colter's taste. Some of the men coming in were Americans, drifters for the most part, looking for excitement or a flashing-eyed señorita to take back home as a wife. They were of all ages but predominantly twenties to late thirties.

A young Texan noticed Colter sitting by himself and came over with a bottle of tequila and a shaker of salt. He carried a Winchester carbine under one arm. "Can I buy you a drink, pardner?"

Colter studied the young, alert face. It reminded him a little of his brother Jack. He smiled. "Sure. Have a seat."

The Texan sat and poured two drinks. Then he set the Winchester on the table and handed a glass to Colter. When Colter accepted it, the Texan extended his hand.

"Name's Paul McCay but my friends call me Cody."

"Well, Cody," Colter said, shaking his hand, "it's good to know you. Mine's Colter Haines from up Charleston way."

At that moment Duke entered with another man, and

they walked to the bar. Cody studied Colter's reaction to Duke's entrance.

"You must know that fella."

"Yeah," Colter said, "you could say that. I came to take him back to Charleston for murder or bury him here. The choice is his."

"You a lawman?"

"Nope! He killed my kid brother and four others."

"The kind of neighbor everybody wants," Cody said, smiling. "You want some help?"

"I think I can take him all right, but thanks," Colter said. He got up and eased the loop off the hammer of his Colt. Then, drawing the weapon, he walked up and shoved it into Duke's back. "Let's go, Duke. I'm taking you back."

Duke was in the act of raising his glass to his mouth when he stopped cold. Then, he slowly completed the movement and swallowed a large gulp of tequila. Setting the glass on the bar, he called out in a loud voice. "This man's packin' a badge. He's a lawman. You fellas gonna let lawmen come in and walk out with anybody they want?"

"Shut up and move, Duke," Colter barked.

"Next time it may be one of you he hauls out of here," Duke shouted.

One young Mexican vaquero rose to his feet behind Colter and shoved his gun into Colter's back. "Drop your gun, gringo."

When Duke heard Colter's gun drop, he spun around, relieved. A grin split his face from side to side. *"Gracias, amigo,"* he said to the vaquero.

"I am not a lawman. He killed my brother, and I came to take him back."

"He's a liar," Duke said, and he hit Colter a glancing blow as Colter ducked. Duke grinned and gazed around at everyone. "He's purty quick, ain't he? Well,

I'll show you what we do to lawmen back home. Let's see if he can duck a bullet.''

A shot rang out and the wood between Duke's feet splintered. Duke kept his hands to his sides. Cody's voice rang out in the silence that followed. ''Hey, vaquero, you want to see which one of us can shoot the fastest?''

The vaquero who had his gun in Colter's back glanced over at Cody and found himself staring down the muzzle of a Winchester. He licked his lips dryly, dropped his gun, and raised his hands slowly so there would be no doubt as to his actions.

Cody turned his attention to Duke. ''All right, *big* man. You've done a lot of crowin' about how you treat lawmen where you come from. I imagine they're always facin' the other way when you shoot 'em.''

''You're doin' some crowin' yourself, junior, since you've got the edge with that rifle. How good would you be man to man?''

''I'll tell you, chubby, I want you to face Colter here first, since he was in line before I was. If you survive, which I'm inclined to doubt, I'll take you on with one hand tied behind my back. Colter, pick up your gun and you can start from scratch.''

Colter picked up his gun and slipped it back into its holster. ''All right, Duke, I'm takin' you back to Charleston.''

The people in the cantina scattered, knocking over chairs and spilling drinks in their haste to get out of range of the coming gunfight.

Duke stood snearing at Colter. A smirk spread slowly across his face. ''I don't think you're big enough, Haines.''

''If you don't come along peacefully, I'll have to kill you.''

Duke laughed. ''I've taken better men than you.''

Colter smiled. ''Yeah, but it's different when you

have to look at their guns and not their backs." His goading worked.

Duke drew in anger, and as soon as he grabbed his gun, he knew he had been beaten. Colter's hand was a blur of speed. His big Colt seemed to have made the jump from holster to hand without any visible movement in between. The shot, a thunderous crash inside the confines of the cantina, sent the slug slamming into Duke's big chest about where the sternum holds part of the rib cage together. Its power drove Duke backward before his gun could clear leather. He landed flat, backside down, on the hard, rough floor. His eyes took on that faraway look for a second before they rolled upward, leaving only the white underside visible.

Colter glanced quickly around the sea of faces starting to show themselves above overturned tables. He saw nothing threatening, so he holstered his Colt. Then, turning to Cody, he said, "I'm glad you decided not to listen to what I said about not needin' any help. I'm in your debt."

"Forget it."

"Hardly. If you're ever ridin' through the Charleston area, look me up. I'll be mighty glad to see you."

"Just where is Charleston?"

"About ten miles southwest of Tombstone."

Cody smiled. "I just might do that."

Colter spoke to the bartender. "You bury him, and you can have his things."

The bartender grinned. *"Gracias, señor."*

Colter stuck out his hand. "Thanks again, Cody You gonna be okay here?" He gave a slight nod to ward the vaquero Cody had disarmed.

Cody grinned. "We'll be old buddies in another te minutes. Say that's quite a draw you have, Colter. On of the slickest I've seen." He shook Colter's out stretched hand. "Good luck on your ride back to Charleston."

"*Adiós*," Colter said. He stepped out into the hot midday sun and untied his roan. Suddenly he felt ten years younger. Charleston was only a two day ride, and then . . . Cynthia would be waiting.

ABOUT THE AUTHOR

Quint Wade was born in a migrant camp during the Great Depression. His father was a cowboy and his mother was a ranch cook. Wade grew up hearing stories from cowboys and farmers as his family rode freight trains, lived under bridges, and mined gold in northern California. He now lives in San Diego, California.